This collection of short stories is dedicated

    To three dogs I've loved and lost:

To Chow
Snatched from a cardboard box,
Our first family dog and a rescue.
I grieve that in the rough and tumble of life
We didn't have more time for you.

Maximus Aurelius
You were a Paws with a Cause reject.
Never mind – you were the best therapy dog ever!
You were magnificent in every way.
There'll never be another dog like you – never!

Maggie May (of Rod Stewart fame)
You died when you were seven,
You left us much too soon.
You were the light, the love of my life,
You died on the waning moon.

and to our new Welsh, Snack:
To own a pet makes one vulnerable,
But what's a pet lover to do?
Go out and get another dog of course–
A Welsh named Snackeroo!

"When I look into the eyes of a dog I don't see an animal. I see a living being. I see a friend. I feel a soul." A.D. Williams

TWEETS
A TWITTER FEED
OF
SHORT STORIES

Janet Hasselbring

Contents

Tweets
A Twitter Feed of Short Stories

The Title:

1. Tweets

a. A tweet is the chirp of a bird. *Tweets* seemed a fitting title for this book, since the chapters "For the Birds," and "The Stories behind the Stories," describe interesting habits and fascinating behaviors of birds, including their calls, songs, and chirps.

b. A tweet is also a post made on the social media app, Twitter. A Tweet is a short burst of communication, giving the writer a limit, of 140 characters, to tell their message or sum up what is going on in their life. When you read someone's tweet – a Twitter message – you're reading a burst of truth about their life, activities, observations, and philosophies, summed up in 140 characters or less. The short stories found in this collection, are longer than 140 words/characters; however, they too are limited (see Foreword), and in that sense they are like tweets – short bursts of communication.

2. Twitters

a. A twitter is the call of a bird consisting of repeated, light, tremulous sounds.

b. Twitter is also a social networking site that allows users to write short posts, known as tweets. Since this is a collection of stories or tweets, a twitter feed seemed an appropriate title.

The cover design:

The birds on the cover, the red-eyed vireo and the cowbird, are featured in *Can We Nest Here?*, Book 7, *Tales from Pelican Cove*. They are the creation of Bruce De Vries, a self-taught artist, who works from his home studio in West Michigan. He is the landscape design artist for Fruitport Schools, Fruitport, Michigan. When he isn't working and illustrating children's books, you can usually find him, at work, in his garden.

The photos:

Many of the photos used in "For the Birds," and "Stories behind the Stories," are used with permission from Terry O'Brien and Larry Monat. The photo of the barn and silo on title page, Chapter 2, is used with permission from Jim Schmidt.

TWEETS
A Twitter Feed of Short Stories

ISBN 978-0-578-81674-6
Copyright © 2020 by Janet Hasselbring

*A NAMPA (North American Mature Publishers Association) prize winner

**NAMPA and Maranatha Christian Writer's conference, award winner

***Tate Publisher's award winner

Foreward "Omit Useless Words!"

I wrote the stories in this collection for a national award-winning publication, Senior Perspectives Newspapers (SPN).* I started writing for SPN in 2015 and never looked back. I fell in love with the short story.

I hope you enjoy reading the stories as much as I've enjoyed writing them.

Writing the short story provides me an outlet for the constant stream of ideas flowing through my head – thoughts about gardening, birds, memories of life on the family farm (present-day Country Dairy), travels, and observations generated by books and poems I'm reading.

Writing gives me a sense of wonder and respect for words. Emily Dickinson writes:

> "A word is dead
> When it is said (*written*),
> Some say.
> I say it just
> Begins to live
> That day." (Change mine with apologies to Dickinson.)

"Dipping her pen in a dark inkwell, Dickinson wrote words. A word, say the name of a flower-like 'rose,' became a construct – part memory, part imagination. Imbedded in a poem, with meter and rhyme, words became like the petals of a rose, each different but creating a rhythm and a symmetry." *Emily Dickinson's Gardening Life*, Marta McDowell

Incidentally, this is an example of how readings inspire, impact, and enrich my writing.

Stephen King wisely noted, "To write is human; to edit divine." The writing gods knew what they were doing when they decreed a word limit for the short story. We, writers, are notorious for falling in love with our words, and when writing a first draft, we're encouraged to get our ideas down without worrying about editing them.

Then comes the fun part! Paring a couple hundred words from a story is a challenge, but it's also the most enjoyable part of writing for me.

"Rule Seventeen. Omit needless words!" cautioned Wm Strunk, Jr. *The Elements of Style*. He said it three times to make the case for cleanliness, accuracy, and brevity in the use of English. Strunk's pupil and admirer, E.B. White, whose writing *The New Yorker, Charlotte's Web*, was known for its ease and clarity, wrote a Fourth Edition of his work, which has become every serious writer's "bible." White describes the professor's dedication to his own rule:

"In the days when I was sitting in his class, he omitted so many needless words, and omitted them so forcibly and with such eagerness and obvious relish, that he often seemed in the position of having shortchanged himself – a man left with nothing more to say, yet with time to fill, a radio prophet who had out-distanced the clock. He got out of this predicament by a simple trick: he uttered every sentence three times! Delivering his oration to his class, he leaned forward over his desk, grasped his coat lapels in his hands, and in a husky, conspiratorial voice, muttered, 'Omit needless words. 'Omit needless words. Omit needless words!'" *Elements of Style, 4th Edition*

Luckily for you, my readers, SPN editors enforce word limits and Rule Seventeen is my goal, sparing you "needless words" in the hunt for simplicity and clarity. E.B. White puts it best:

"Strunk felt that readers were in serious trouble most of the time, floundering in a swamp and that it was the duty of anyone attempting to write English to drain this swamp quickly and get the reader on dry ground, or at least throw a rope." *Elements of Style, 4th Edition*, White.

I'm finished. The word count, as usual, is far over the maximum allowed. Excuse me while I delete some useless words! Be right back!

Whew! I made it! On to publication!

Note 1 – Many of the birds' names are in lower case to give the book a more informal look.

Note 2 – Scripture verses are from the Revised Standard Version.

Note 3 – The reader may detect some duplication of material in the Waterfowl series and the companion articles, Teacher Alert/Albert Einstein. Since SPN articles are written six times yearly to unspecified readers, even though the articles are a series or companion pieces, each one has to be able to stand on its own.

*www.SeniorResourcesWMi.org

Chapter 1
Reflections on To a Waterfowl

"Clever man is a chicken; it can fly, but a little. Genius is a migratory bird; it can fly at high altitudes until He disappears on the horizon." Mehmet Muvat IIdan

Roseate Spoonbills

Introduction – Life as a Shorebird

"At whatever moment you read these words, day or night, there are birds aloft in the skies of the Western Hemisphere, migrating." Weidensaul, *Living on the Wind*

As the hot lazy days of summer transition into the crisp cooler days of autumn, over 5 billion birds, mostly unseen by us, will fling themselves into the wind and fly overhead.

William Cullen Bryant's allegorical poem, "*To a Waterfowl*," describes a shorebird's migratory flight and reminds us that our lives, too, are migratory journeys, similar to that of the shorebirds and songbirds aloft in the skies.

"Whither, 'midst falling dew,
While glow the heavens with the last steps of day,
Far, through their rosy depths, dost thou pursue
Thy solitary way?

Vainly the fowler's eye
Might mark thy distant flight, to do thee wrong,
As, darkly seen against the crimson sky,
Thy figure floats along.

Seek'st thou the plashy brink
Of weedy lake, or marge of river wide,
Or where the rocking billows rise and sink
On the chaféd ocean side?

There is a Power, whose care
Teaches thy way along that pathless coast, –
The desert and illimitable air
Lone wandering, but not lost.

All day thy wings have fanned,
At that far height, the cold thin atmosphere;
Yet stoop not, weary, to the welcome land,
Though the dark night is near.

And soon that toil shall end,
Soon shalt thou find a summer home, and rest,
And scream among thy fellows; reeds shall bend,
Soon, o'er thy sheltered nest.

Thou'rt gone, the abyss of heaven
Hath swallowed up thy form, yet, on my heart
Deeply hath sunk the lesson thou hast given,
And shall not soon depart.

He, who, from zone to zone,
Guides through the boundless sky thy certain flight,
In the long way that I must trace alone,
Will lead my steps aright." William Cullen Bryant

This series will explore Bryant's poem verse by verse, seeking what wisdom we can glean from the shorebird. My mother, Ellen, will be the speaker in the poem. As the poem is, in essence, a profession of faith, her musings are a testimony to her life of faith on a small farm, in the 1930s, where she and her beloved Henry eked out a living, raised their children, and honed their faith. Her life of faith and surrender to the will of God is documented in the memoir, *In the Garden.*

Guided by the stars, the sun, by crystals in their little birdbrains, by landmarks, and by following a path graven in their genes, these amazing avian fliers undertake long arduous journeys to their winter feeding grounds. Their flights are examples of perseverance, determination, and pure grit:

When the ruddy turnstones take to the wind, from the Arctic mudflats and journey to their winter homes in Patagonia, they will fly 5 to 8 days at a time, without food and water. Their wings will flap a total of 3,000,000 times in their quest for food. When they return north in the spring, they will have flown approximately 18,000 miles (see map).

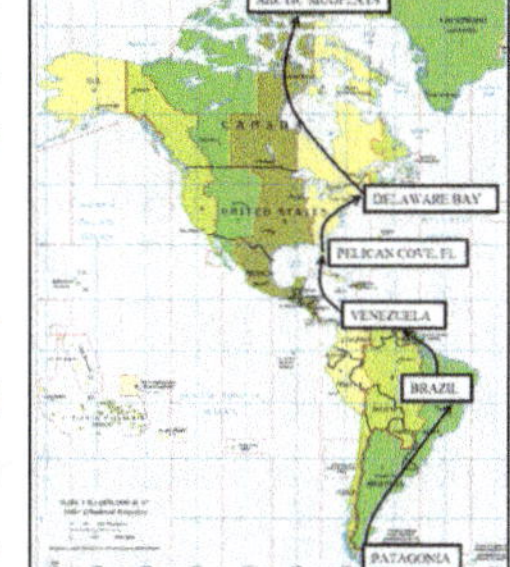

The red knot, on its way north from Patagonia to Delaware Bay, flies over the bulge of Brazil for 10 days straight – a 240-hour trip, without stopping for food or water. This plucky flier, banded B95, is nicknamed the Moonbird because in his 20 plus years of migrating, he's flown the equivalent mileage of traveling to the moon and back. The oldest red knot, B95, has become an icon for birders.

The white-rumped sandpiper flies 9000 miles twice each year pursuing summer. That was a record until birders banded and logged the arctic tern. What they found was astonishing:

This 4 ounce wonder flies, 44,000 miles round trip, from Nova Scotia across the Atlantic to the southern shores of Africa, back over the Atlantic to Patagonia, back to Africa, then back over the ocean for the fourth time to Nova Scotia and from there to the Arctic mudflats – a dazzling aerial figure eight in pursuit of food.

The blackpoll warbler is one of the gustiest songbirds. This little sprite starts out from Alaska and flies 3000 miles east to Nova Scotia, where he gorges on webworms and sawflies. When a strong NW wind blows, he's off on a 2000-mile transoceanic flight. A mere 4" long and weighing one-third of an ounce (that's 50 birds to the pound!), he's all feathers, hollow bones, and heart. Since he cannot swim, he must keep flying – up to 90 hours at a time! He doesn't glide, so if he's not flapping, he's dropping. On long flights, he sprints forward, folds back his wings, and drops – over and over again – 20 times a minute.

Migratory birds fly mostly at night when the air is less turbulent and they waste less energy. The cooler air diffuses dangerously high levels of body heat from the constant flapping and reduces dehydration. Enemies, particularly, hawks, are diurnal, and owls, though night prowlers, aren't agile enough to harm them. Flying against incredible odds, including dehydration, starvation, disease, predators, skyscrapers lit up at night, and satellite towers that can take out unwitting fliers, their GPS systems take them back and forth to the same spots every year!

This is the shorebird Bryant memorializes in his poem, *To a Waterfowl.*

In the Garden: an Ordinary Woman; An Extraordinary Life, Ellen – A Memoir, is a testimony to the power of faith and surrender to God's will. The author recounts the story of her mother, Ellen, who, during times of suffering and loss, met her Lord, "in the garden," and asked, "Lord, what would You have me do?" Putting down roots with Henry, her husband, on a small farm in western MI (site of present-day Country Dairy, www.country-dairy.com), Ellen found the where and wherefore of God's plan for her life. There, on the farm, in the house on the hill, this ordinary woman surrendered her life to the will of her Lord. The author realizes that the secret of her mother's life and her peaceful, victorious death was that "she died before she died."

Great Blue Heron

Verse 1 – A Pair of Cardinals

"At whatever moment you read these words, day or night, there are birds aloft in the skies of the Western Hemisphere, migrating." *Living on the Wind*, Weidensaul

"Whither, 'midst falling dew,
While glows the heavens with the last steps of day,
Far, through their rosy depths, dost thou pursue
Thy solitary way?" *To a Waterfowl*, Wm Cullen Bryant

In Bryant's beloved poem, the speaker addresses a shorebird in flight:

"As dew falls and the sun sets in the rosy depths of the heavens, where you are going?"

As the waterfowl begins its journey, it can't possibly know what challenges and difficulties it may encounter along the way. Likewise, Ellen couldn't possibly have known what life held in store for her when she married the love of her life, Henry, and began a new life on the farm.

In this series on Bryant's masterpiece, my mother, Ellen, is the speaker in the poem. As the poem is, at heart, a profession of faith, her musings are a testimony to her life of faith on the small farm in the 1930s, where she, and her beloved Hinie, eked out a living, raised their children, and honed their faith.

"Nothing in Ellen's life, growing up in a comfortable, well-to-do home in the city, could have prepared her for the stark reality of living on (and off) the land; still she threw herself into her new life with determination and optimism, for she loved Henry with all her heart and was committed to their life together.

The farm is bleak in March. A grim austere landscape greeted Ellen in mid/late March as she and Henry returned from their honeymoon and settled into their new home. Looking out the kitchen window on her first morning on the farm she would have seen the sun rising to the east. Barren scraggy trees were scattered here and there in the yard. Sooty stale piles of snow were reminders of winter's frigid blast.

Patches of green dotting the snow-covered pasture and a ring of water circling the frozen pond were hopeful signs that the bleak barrenness would not last forever. The pond wound lazily uphill to the woods – a scruffy, scraggly army of trees guarding the rear boundary. She might have seen the cows, relieved of their saggy udders, straggling out in a line to greet the first signs of spring, following their leader to seek what sustenance they could find in the grim austere wilderness of the pasture. As she waited for Henry to return from his early milking for breakfast, her sense of excitement and exuberance shifted to a twinge of uncertainty and doubt, triggered, perhaps, by the foreboding scene framed in the kitchen window. Suddenly, she felt vulnerable, alone, and unsure of herself. What was she doing here? She knew nothing of farm life or being a farm wife. Her comfortable, leisurely life back home, only one and a half miles away, seemed far away indeed. ...Yet, here she was in the kitchen, dressed in her new house dress and apron, feeling lost and alone. Suddenly a flash of red flew past the window. A male cardinal was perched on a limb in the blue spruce, his shebird a few branches up. A pair of cardinals, she thought. A pair just Henry and me. The sight of the birds lifted her spirits. Henry would be home soon. He would make everything right. She loved him with all her heart. He was a farmer, so she would be his farm wife. Well, a housewife who lives on the farm, she thought. Somehow that sounded better. Ellen started the coffee, set the sausages sizzling, and whipped the pancake batter into a froth. Henry would be home soon. He would be hungry. She had better get busy fixing his breakfast. Ellen's life on the farm had begun." *In the Garden* pp 22, 23

Northern Cardinal

And so it was, on her first morning on the farm, that a pair of cardinals brought hope and reassurance to Ellen. It would not be the only time that Dickinson's "things with feathers," lifted Ellen's spirits and put a song in her heart.

I love the image of my mother, in the kitchen, wearing a new housedress and apron, full of love for Henry, and full of hope and promise for their future together. How could she have known then how dramatically her life would be shaped and fashioned by the farm and, in turn, how indelibly the farm would bear the stamp of her presence? In the beginning, it was her love for Henry that nurtured and sustained her, but as time went on and the challenges of eking out a living and raising a family on the farm increased, that love would find new meaning and strength in their shared faith in God and His Word.

"I know the plans I have for you," says the Lord, "plans for good and not for evil, to give you a future and a hope." *Jeremiah 29:11*

Osprey

Verse 2 – Keeping Danger at Bay

As I write, hunting season is on. Deer graze in peril, pheasants scoot in and out of sparse piles of brush, migrating shorebirds fly exposed against a cloudless sky – all of them fighting the odds against hunters, in camouflage, who would do them harm. Hunting dogs bark or "bay" at game until their masters can arrive on the scene. "Keeping at bay" can also mean to keep something or someone stopped awhile until help arrives.

The annual exchange between hunters and unsuspecting prey is described by William Cullen Bryant in verse two of his poem, *To a Waterfowl*:

"Vainly the fowler's eye
Might mark thy distant flight to do thee wrong,
As, darkly painted on the crimson sky,
Thy figure floats along."

Migration, for a shorebird, is a challenging enterprise – dehydration, lack of food, veering off course, battling wind currents, and always, the feared fowler – all pose threats for the shorebird.

My parents also faced challenges. Living and working on a small farm in west Michigan symbolizes their migratory journey:

Eking out a living…

"A sick cow contaminates and ruins the entire day's milk. Too little rain and newly planted seeds suffocate; too much and they wash away. A windstorm destroys the annual cherry crop…" *In the Garden*, pg. 32

Losing a daughter…

"When my sister died, my mother was stunned beyond belief. As she struggled to comprehend the incomprehensible and accept the unacceptable, her spirit sagged and slowly ebbed away. She appeared dazed and lifeless. Finally, paralyzed by grief, she withdrew to her room." *In the Garden*, pg. 65

Estrangement...

How could my mother have known that when she sent her youngest son to the jungles of Viet Nam, her relationship with him would be changed forever? "To her dying day, she held out hope she would see or hear from him one last time, but it was not to be..." *In the Garden*, pg. 75

The shorebird eluded the hunter's gun. My parents eluded danger too – not death, necessarily, but despair, disillusionment, bitterness, resentment, and hopelessness, which for us, humans, are worse conditions than death, because they affect eternity.

Through Scripture, prayer, and surrender, they chose faith, hope, love, acceptance, and surrender to God's will over their own.

"Faith is what God asks of us. His invisibility is the test of faith. To know who sees Him, God makes Himself invisible." *Unbroken*, Hillenbrand

"Their faith enabled them to see life beyond the cornfields, the cherry orchards, the clothesline, and the garden, and helped them through the disappointments of a blighted cherry crop, rotted potatoes, diseased cows, and sick children..." *In the Garden* pg. 74

My parents joined the ranks of spiritual greats, who throughout history, in the face of great loss, illness, imprisonment, or impending death, accepted the seemingly unacceptable, thereby finding, the "peace that passeth all understanding."

"Their lives were taken up into the great plan of God, where, like the fragments of broken glass, they glowed with immortal meaning in the design of His grand mosaic." *The Story of the Psalms*, Van Dyke

"...thy figure floats along."

Great White Egret

Verse 3 – Warm Weather, No Traffic, No Deadlines, No Queues!

"Seek'st thou the plashy brink
Of weedy lake, or marge of river wide
Or where the rocking billows rise and sink
Off the chafed ocean side?" *To a Waterfowl,* Wm Cullen Bryant

The sniff of spring is in the air and the snowbirds, human and feathered, are heading home.

In verse 3, my mother, Ellen, the travel agent, is planning her client's (the waterfowl's) trip to an idyllic destination in the great out-of-doors, promising him, on his solitary way, the best views, the finest accommodations, and the cheapest rates, unfettered by traffic, deadlines, or queues. To snowbirds, in Florida, this sounds like paradise!

My mother loved birds. She was enchanted by the full-throated ease of their singing and their effortless freedom of flight. She came from wealth and luxury, but when she met Henry, the love of her life, and moved to the farm, her life changed dramatically. Though she never looked back or questioned her decision, I can't help but wonder, when life, as Henry's helpmeet and homemaker, came at her hard (and it often did), if she viewed "things with feathers" with a twinge of envy.

Ellen loved traveling; however, during the early years on the farm, daily chores, and caring for children, made it difficult for my parents to get away. Everywhere they went, we went too – nine of us jouncing along in the turquoise and black Plymouth sedan. Seat belts had yet to be invented. I perched on the edge of the front seat, in between my mother and

Great White Egret

big sister; the remaining five vied for the window seats in the back. Off we went leaving our comfort zone for the big world beyond.

These getaways couldn't have been pleasant for Ellen. A noisy rambunctious brood within the confines of a car was definitely a migraine in the making.

In the summer, when our chores were done and time allowed, my mother would take us, girls, to Lake Michigan. Was it then, as she watched us play and the seagulls swooping and diving overhead, she felt an urge for freedom?

As we grew older, their trips matured – rides in the countryside, watching sunsets over Lake Michigan, spiritual retreats at Maranatha and Winona Lake, Indiana, visiting their children living out of state, and winter visits to Ellen's parents in Florida.

In 1968, my father sold the farm to his son, Wendell, and for the first time, since their honeymoon in March, 1936, my parents were unencumbered by daily chores, child rearing, or financial worries. Ellen's wanderlust longings were fulfilled, and though my father's favorite place was in the living room or on the front porch, he traveled the world with my mother.

"Seek'st thou…?"

Through it all – from early on, when she sat on the front porch, breastfeeding a newborn or watching a bird in flight, to the days when her yen for travel was realized, Ellen trusted her Lord and her calling to the place where she put down her roots.

"Ellen felt a fluttering within, like a brace of birds, longing to be free. Free! Oh, how she longed to be free. Free from the woes that beset them – free from the lack of money, free from dreaded windblight, free from sick cows and contaminated milk, free from insufficient rain]and parched earth, free from accidents… Free! The flutterings increased until, like a wave, her fears rose up inside and nearly engulfed her. She could scarcely breathe. It felt like her heart would burst. Then, with a sudden surge, the wave erupted and like a bird, on the wing, her soul felt light and free. She stood in stunned relief, a stab of joy pierced her heart. In spite of everything, joy! Just as her Lord had promised…" *In the Garden*, pg. 56

Yellow-crowned Night Heron

Verse 4 – Life, A Dash

"There is a power whose care
Teaches thy way along that pathless coast
The desert and illimitable air,
Lone, wandering, but not lost." *To a Waterfowl*, Wm Cullen Bryant

My mother's gravestone bears this designation: "Amazing Grace. Dec 8, 1914 - Sept 1, 2005." I gaze at the combination of numbers and letters that summarize my mother's life. I marvel that a single dash set between the dates of her birth and death, can somehow comprise her life.

"For you created my inmost being; you knit me together in my mother's womb..." *Psalm 139:13 - 15*

In his poem, *To a Waterfowl*, Bryant reminds us that the dash (which will be found on each of our gravestones), symbolizes a migratory journey, starting with our first gasp of air and ending with the last. One grand pilgrimage with many and various secondary trips throughout.

Yellow-crowned Night Heron

The one secondary experience that would define my mother's pilgrimage was marrying my father, Henry, and moving to the little farm in west MI, to the house on the hill, where they lived together for over sixty years.

"Nothing in Ellen's life, growing up in a comfortable, well-to-do home in the city, could have prepared her for the stark reality of living on (and off) the land; still, she threw herself into her new life with determination and optimism, for she loved Henry with all her heart and was totally committed to their life together." *In the Garden*, pg. 22

"There is a power whose care..."

My parents grew up in Christian homes, attended Sunday school, and publicly professed their faith; however, as I write in my mother's memoir, *In the Garden*, their faith was honed on the farm, becoming deeply personal through the challenges of making a living and raising their family.

When did my mother first become aware of "a power that would teach her way..."? When did she come to know the presence of God?

"On a crisp Monday morning in mid-April (1938), Ellen had just pinned her last bed sheet onto the clothesline, when a black-capped chickadee perched on a branch overhead, trilling its heart out. 'Oh you beautiful creature,' Ellen called. Something about that plump little bird lifted her spirits and gave her a burst of hope.

Black-capped Chickadee

She felt a longing deep within; an awakening to nature and the power of the birds' singing, trees budding, breezes blowing, and clothes flapping in the wind. Was it then she knew "a power" beyond all that she could see, smell, hear, and feel?

God was in the chickadee's song. As she listened, the worries and cares that weighed on her heart, like a brace of birds, were lifted, and like a bird on the wing, they vanished into the air. With God's help, she could meet any challenge..." *In the Garden*, pp. 27, 28

"Lone, wandering, but not lost..."

"Where can I go from your Spirit? Where can I flee from your presence? If I go up to the heavens, you are there; if I make my bed in the depths, you are there. If I rise on the wings of dawn, if I settle on the far side of the sea, even there your hand will guide me, your right hand will hold me fast." *Psalm 139: 7 - 10*

I gaze at her gravestone and hear the words of the psalmist:

"All the days ordained for me were written in your book before one of them came to be." *Psalm 139:16*

Pelican

Verse 5 – All the Way to Lake Michigan

"All day thy wings have fanned,
At that far height, the cold thin atmosphere;
Yet stoop not, weary, to the welcome land,
Though the dark night is near." *To a Waterfowl*, Wm Cullen Bryant

"Our home had a front porch, where my parents used to sit, in the cool of the evening, after their chores were done. Here they communed with nature, beat tired, but happy and content after a hard day's work. Long after the sun set over the western hills, they enjoyed the cool breezes, listened to the crickets singing, and the frogs croaking. On a clear day, my father claimed he could see all the way to Lake Michigan." *In the Garden*, pp 50, 51

Now it was approximately a 30-minute drive from our house to the Big Lake, and in between there were many hills, curves in the road, fields of corn and alfalfa, and apple and cherry orchards. It would take some doing to see past all of that to the sparkling blue waters of Lake Michigan, but my father knew the lake would be there at the end of the drive.

It seems my father's claim was one more of faith than reality; more symbol than fact. To me, his claim is a metaphor of my parents' faith: just as my father claimed he could see all the way to Lake Michigan on a clear day, so firm was my parents' faith, they believed they could "see" all the way to heaven from their house on the hill on their small farm in western Michigan.

My parents' lives were founded and grounded on the Scriptures and prayer. As they went about their chores – plowing the fields, fixing the fences, hanging out the clothes, or weeding the roses, the truths contained in the Scriptures became real to them and the mysteries of the infinite unfolded within their souls.

Their faith was strengthened through life's experiences, giving them hope and comfort in the midst of trials, disappointments, and challenges. When life on the farm came at them hard, and it often did, "their faith enabled them to see past the cornfields, the cherry orchards, the clothesline, and the garden, to see life beyond. Their faith helped them see through the disappointments of a blighted cherry crop, rotted potatoes, diseased cows, and a sick child. Faith helped them to see, at the end of it all, their eternal inheritance." *In the Garden*, pg. 118

Their faith was not an ostrich-like escapism or childish wishful thinking. Not at all. The more they looked "all the way to heaven," the more seriously they took their earthly responsibilities; however, with heaven in mind, they worked, loved, cared, and struggled with a new dimension – at the end of a hard day's toil, they turned everything over to God.

According to C.S. Lewis, "Hope is one of the theological virtues. This means that a continual looking forward to the eternal world is one of the things a Christian is meant to do....If you read history, you will find that those who did most for the present world, thought most of the next....Aim at heaven and you will get earth thrown in; aim at earth and you will get neither." Lewis, *Christian Behavior*

Emmet Fox writes, "Heaven lies all about us – it is not a distinct locality afar off in the skies, but all around us now. Heaven is the religious name for the Presence of God; Heaven is infinite; Heaven is Eternity; Heaven is the realm of Spirit... To 'see' God is to apprehend Truth as it really is, and this is infinite freedom and perfect bliss." Fox, *Sermon on the Mount*

The challenges on the farm were many: if a cow got sick, the entire day's supply of milk would be contaminated and would have to be dumped; too little rain would suffocate newly planted seeds, while a downpour would wash them away; an untimely windstorm could destroy the cherry crop, and to make matters worse, Henry would have to pay to have the cherries picked and dumped to ensure a healthy crop the next year.

Henry was used to the vicissitudes and vulnerabilities of farming; however, it was Ellen, a farm fledgling, who became his comforter in times of adversity.

"Henry stands at the dining room window, watching the windstorm wreak havoc on his cherry crop. The entire crop is ruined. His shoulders convulse with sobs. *How will we pay our bills?* he wonders. Ellen has not a clue how they will manage. 'Don't worry, honey,' she says stoutly, 'God will provide.'" *In the Garden*, pg. 94

"God will provide," became their mantra. And, He did. As the house on the hill was built on a firm foundation, their faith was honed on a daily diet of scripture and prayer.

Like a muscle, their faith was exercised daily; stretching, growing, and becoming as strong as the rocks turned over by the plow in the field; their trust in God as sure as the sun that rose and set daily, their walk with God as straight and narrow as the furrows formed by the plow Henry held as he walked back and forth across the fields behind the workhorses, Maude and Daize." *In the Garden*, pg. 33

...see all the way to Lake Michigan; see all the way to Heaven. What a marvelous confession of faith.

"...Stoop not, weary, to the welcome land,
though the dark of night is near."

Arctic Tern

Verse 6 – I'll Fly Away

"And soon that toil shall end.
Soon shalt thou find a summer home and rest,
And scream among thy fellows; reeds shall bend
Soon, o'er thy sheltered nest." *To a Waterfowl,* Wm Cullen Bryant

Timing. It's everything. I couldn't have known when I began this series, comparing Bryant's depiction of the shorebird's migration to the pilgrimage of my mother, Ellen, that Verse 6, describing the shorebird's arrival at the safety and shelter of his summer home, would be published in the September issue of Senior Perspectives. My mother reached her "summer home," on September 1, 2005. Coincidences are moments when little shafts of light break through the monotony and normal parameters of our days. I'm sure I miss a lot of them. Not this one.

Late August 2005: Helpless and dying, Ellen rests on the hospital bed, which Hospice has set up in the living room. She gazes out over the farmland to the hills beyond. A sense of eternity pervades the room.

I listen in on her final conversation, "in the garden," with her Lord:

"Ellen," The voice is familiar, soft, and so tender. "My Lord is it You calling?" "Yes, Ellen, it is time." "Time?" She seemed puzzled. "Is it time for me to get up, my Lord? I think I have overslept. I have work to do – beans to snip, roses to tend, socks to darn," she rushes on.

"No my dear one. You have fought the good fight. You have run the race. Your earthly chores are done. It is time to go. Today your name will be called by the One who formed you in the beginning of time."

As His words break through to her, hardly daring to believe their meaning, she whispers, "My Lord, can it be true? I have waited so long for this moment?"

"Ellen, today you will enter into the joy of your Lord. Come, the angels are waiting to bring you home. Can you hear them singing?" *In the Garden*, pg. 109

"Soon thy toil shall end…"

A shorebird's migratory journey is fraught with dangers. Besides looking out for prowling predators or human "fowlers," our bird requires a plentiful food supply, energy for flying thousands of miles, and an internal GPS system that will keep him on course.

So, too, for Ellen, eking out a living on a small farm with Henry, had its perils. Infected cows, untimely winds, and torrential downpours, resulted in heart-rending losses. The death of a daughter, who died too soon, and estrangement from a son, who survived the jungles of Viet Nam, but never returned home, tore at the fabric of Ellen's soul. In these "why" moments, Ellen found her Lord, "in the garden." On the small farm in west Michigan, my parents were caught up in the great plan of God, which gave their lives an eternal beauty and dignity.

Sitting with my mother, as she traveled back and forth on the road to Heaven, inspired me to write her story. As she drifted in and out of consciousness, she would awaken from her dozing and be talking, lucidly, with Henry {my father}, and though I couldn't see him, he was obviously there for her." *In the Garden*, pg. 106

My mother's voice, ever so faint, brings me back to the present…

"Angels, my Lord? Yes, I hear them. I see them in the distance. They are coming closer. And someone is with them." Joy rushing forth like a geyser from the ground. "Can it be, yes it is. It's my Henry! I am ready, my Lord! I am ready to go home." *In the Garden*, pg. 109

I have no doubt my father was sent to accompany my mother home at the time of her death.

"Oh, that I had the wings of a dove! I would fly away and be at rest." *Psalm 55:6*

Arctic Terns in Arctic mudflats

Brown Pelican

Verse 7 – *Her* Children Rise Up and Call her Blessed

"Thou'rt gone, the abyss of heaven
Hath swallowed up thy form, yet, on my heart
Deeply hath sunk the lesson thou hast given,
And shall not soon depart." *To a Waterfowl*, Wm Cullen Bryant

In the memoir, *In the Garden*, I describe the times I spent with my mother at the end of her life. Those weren't her best years, health-wise, but those *kairos* moments, charged with eternity, changed my life.

I sat at her bedside, mesmerized, as she lay dying. I listened in as she traveled back and forth on the pathway to Heaven, talking, lucidly, with those who had gone on before into heaven. I listened in amazement, as she talked with Henry, my father, who was also in heaven, yet, was somehow there in the room. I felt I was on holy ground. I'm certain it was at that time, I knew I would write her story.

"On the morning my mother died, funeral home attendants prepared to take her body away. The house was eerily still, deafeningly quiet; the life snuffed out of the house on the hill. I knew she had flown away to her heavenly home, where she was free of pain and sorrow, but I didn't want her to go. A voice, from somewhere deep inside of me, thundered, 'No! No!'" *In the Garden*, pp. 109, 110

My cry echoed at the funeral. "At the internment, we stood staring at the gaping hole that would hold her earthly remains of our mother, grandmother, and great grandmother. Suddenly, a child's cry pierced the air. One of my niece's daughters, in a sudden realization of the finality of death, voiced our collective feelings, 'No! We don't want you to go!' Shovelfuls of sand heaped on the lowered casket reminded us that she was gone from us and the house on the hill forever. We were left to mourn her absence in our lives." *In the Garden*, pg. 112

C.S. Lewis describes the sobering significance of losing one's mother:

"With my mother's death, all settled happiness,
All that was tranquil and reliable disappeared from my life.
There was to be fun, many pleasures, many stabs of joy,
But no more of the old security.
It was sea and island now.
The great continent had sunk like Atlantis."
A Grief Observed, Lewis

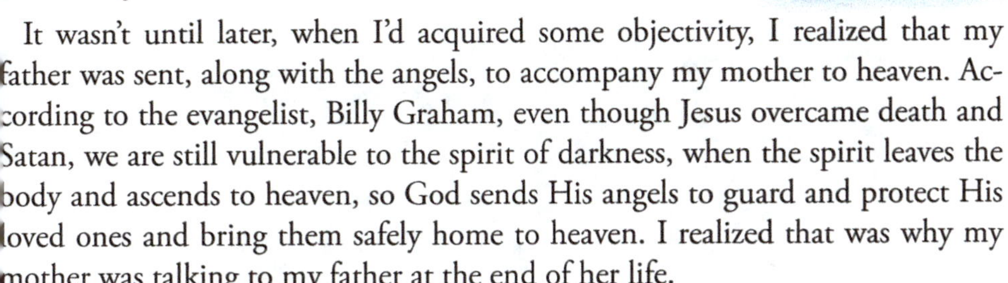

It wasn't until later, when I'd acquired some objectivity, I realized that my father was sent, along with the angels, to accompany my mother to heaven. According to the evangelist, Billy Graham, even though Jesus overcame death and Satan, we are still vulnerable to the spirit of darkness, when the spirit leaves the body and ascends to heaven, so God sends His angels to guard and protect His loved ones and bring them safely home to heaven. I realized that was why my mother was talking to my father at the end of her life.

Once, in a far off time and place, Ellen and Henry, after becoming man and wife, walked down the aisle together. Now I picture them, once again, arm in arm, entering the pearly gates of heaven, together forever in eternity.

It was a privilege to have been with my mother during her final days. It made an indelible impression on me. I was determined to share what I had witnessed.

"A memoir is a reflective rearrangement of actual events." Larry Woiwoode

I began to research and gather information. I went deep within her life and attempted to walk in her footsteps. The more I learned, the more I realized that her death was victorious and peaceful because of the way she lived. At every crossroads of her life, when she faced a defining, "why" moment, she chose faith over doubt, hope over despair, acceptance over resignation, good over evil, and love, which has no opposite. She surrendered her ego to the will of her heavenly Father – in a sense, "she died before she died."

As I reflected on her life, the mystique of the last years I spent with her became clearer:

"When I think of my mother, I do not think of her as infirm, frail, or weak. I see a wrinkled worn face creased with a smile of greeting. I remember a serene gentle person radiating beauty and holiness, vibrant peace, and stillness. There was no interruption or distortion blocking the light which beamed from her countenance. The sunshine of God streamed through her; as the sun radiates light, so she radiated love. She had arrived at the place from which her journey had begun." *In the Garden* pg. 135

"Next to the might of God, the serene beauty of a holy life is the most powerful influence for good in the world." Dwight L. Moody

My mother not only taught me how to die; she taught me how to live as well.

"...yet, on my heart
Deeply hath sunk the lesson thou hast given..."

Swans

"Don't stand by my grave and weep,
For I am not there.
I do not sleep.
I am a thousand winds that blow,
I am the diamond's glint on snow,
I am the sunlight on ripened grain,
I am the gentle autumn's rain.
In the soft hush of the morning light
I am the swift bird in flight.
Don't stand by my grave and cry,
I am not there.
I did not die." Unknown Native American author

Ruddy Turnstone

Verse 8 – From Zone to Zone

"He, who, from zone to zone,
Guides through the boundless sky thy certain flight,
In the long way that I must trace alone,
Will lead my steps aright." *To a Waterfowl*, Wm Cullen Bryant

The heavens are silent. The shorebird has reached his summer home, where he will build a nest with his shebird. As the poet ponders his passing, I too stop to ponder the significance of my mother's journey. Her days, from beginning to end, were lived in relationship with her heavenly Father, her faith honed on a daily diet of Scripture and prayer, and many hours spent communing with her Lord in the great cathedral of nature.

I. Sunrise – The Early Years

"All the days ordained for me were written in your book before one of them came to be." *Psalm 139:1*

Though Henry was used to the vicissitudes of farming, it was Ellen, a farm fledgling, who often comforted Henry in the face of adversities.

The challenges of farm life were multiple: if a cow got sick, the entire day's supply of milk was contaminated and would have to be dumped; too little rain would suffocate newly planted seeds; too much would wash them away.An inopportune windstorm could destroy an entire cherry crop, and to make matters worse, Henry would have to pay to have the cherries picked and dumped to ensure a healthy crop the next year.

"Henry stands at the dining room window sobbing as he watches the windstorm wreak havoc on his cherry crop. His entire crop is ruined. "Ruined," he sobs, everything is ruined. How will we pay our bills?" Ellen too wonders how they will manage. "Don't worry, honey," she says. "God will provide."

"God will provide," became her mantra. And He did. As the hill was built on a firm foundation, their faith was honed on a daily diet of scripture, prayer, and communing with God in nature.

"Like a muscle, their faith would be exercised daily, stretching and growing as strong as the rocks turned over by the plow in the field; their trust in God as sure as the sun that rose and set daily overhead; their walk with God as straight and narrow as the furrows formed by the plow Henry held as he walked back and forth across the fields behind the workhorses, Maude and Daize." *In the Garden*, pg. 33

Their faith was honed early on with the physical challenges of eking out a living for their rapidly-growing family; however, two events looming on the horizon would challenge their faith and cause it to be tried in the crucible of tragedy and suffering.

II. Noontime – The Middle Years

"Where can I go from Thy spirit? Where can I flee from Thy presence? If I go up to the heavens, you are there; if I make my bed in the depths, you are there. If I rise on the wings of the dawn, if I settle on the far side of the sea, even there your hand will guide me; your right hand will hold me fast." *Psalm 139: 7*

Turnstone

a. My sister died tragically at the age of 48. When she heard the news, my mother went into shock. If you had hit her outright with a baseball bat, she could not have been more stunned. Struggling to comprehend the incomprehensible, accept the unacceptable, her spirit sagged within her and ebbed slowly away. She appeared dazed and lifeless. Finally, paralyzed by grief and despair, she withdrew to her room, where she remained for several days. I remember passing by her room once, as my father was leaving. She lay, curled up under the bedcovers, facing the windows, like a shroud." *In the Garden*, pg. 65

Besides grieving my sister, we worried about our mother, whether she could survive the death of her beloved daughter. Then, suddenly, she appeared. A definite peace and serenity, almost otherworldly, radiated from her. We were amazed. She attended the funeral, and though quiet and subdued, she carried herself with grace and graciousness, and gave my sister's life and struggle the dignity and respect it deserved.

Reflecting on the time my mother spent in her room, I am convinced she met Jesus there in her grief and sorrow, wrestling with her Lord, until spent and exhausted, she submitted her will to the will of her Heavenly Father.

Her life would never be the same and though she carried her grief to her own grave, the peace and serenity she exhibited after she emerged from her room, stayed with her for the rest of her days.

b. My youngest brother enlisted for Viet Nam, when he was eighteen, just out of high school. My mother could not have known, when she bid him goodbye, that her relationship with him would be altered forever. He survived the jungle of war, but he never returned home. To her dying day, she prayed that she would see him, talk to him before she died, but it was not to be.

What makes this story especially poignant is that my brother was a miracle baby. His pregnancy was difficult from the start. My mother was sick most of the time and then complications led the doctor to advise my parents that if my mother carried this baby to term, she would most certainly die. Imagine the dilemma for my parents. They did not believe in abortion; however, if my mother died in childbirth, how would my father cope with seven children to manage alone?

As they did with every problem, my parents took their dilemma to the Lord in prayer. Trusting in their Lord, my mother carried the baby to full term and my brother was born. He was always special to her – her seventh and last child; an answer to prayer.

Now she mourns for his return. How does a mother live with the realization that a son she carried in her womb and nursed at her breast, rejects her, his family? How many bottles would it take to hold the tears shed in her grief and sorrow?

With Job, she cried out in anguish, "Have pity on me, my friends, have pity, for the hand of God has struck me." *Job 19:21*

She threw herself on the mercies of her Lord and clung to the promises of Scripture. Once again, she wrestled with her Lord and surrendered to the will of her Heavenly Father.

She now prays for the physical and spiritual well-being of her son. She understands that, like many veterans of the war, his experiences in Viet Nam were traumatic and emotionally scarring, making it impossible for him to return to the normalcy of home and family. Realizing that she might not see him on this side of heaven, she prays that they will be reunited in eternity.

Having two sons myself, I can only imagine the pain this estrangement cost my mother. Though this story did not have a happy ending, I can't help but think the whole story has not been told. God, in the end, will have the last word:

"to {her} that overcometh, I will give to eat of the hidden manna and will give {her} a white stone, and on the stone, a new name written, which no one knoweth save {she} that receiveth it." *Revelation 2:17*. I'm so bold as to believe the name written on the stone is my brother's.

Red Knots

Many people who experience tragedy and loss can no longer believe in a God who would allow pain and suffering. This was not the way of my parents. They never forsook their Jesus. They laid their pain at the foot of the cross, where their Lord met them with love and compassion and filled them with acceptance, strength, and grace.

"Faith is what God asks of us. His invisibility is the test of faith. To know who sees Him, God makes Himself invisible." Hillenbrand, *Unbroken*

III. Sunset – The Final Years

"I know that my Redeemer lives and that in the end, He will stand upon the earth…yet in my flesh, will I see God." *Job 19: 25, 26*

In her last years, my mother was homebound, vulnerable, and virtually helpless; however, I do not remember her as frail, weak, or infirm. She radiated serenity, peace, holiness, and transparence. It was as though the sunshine of God's presence was shining through her. To be with her was to be on holy ground.

My mother died a gentle, humble, emptied child of God, but death was not the end for her. Watching her, fearlessly face the final enemy – Death, changed my life, and over time, was the impetus for writing her memoir.

Like these biblical giants, her faith was tested in the crucible of suffering:

a. Jacob – Like Jacob of old, who wrestled with God at Peniel, my mother wrestles with her Lord, surrendering to His will, when she withdraws to her room, after my sister died.

b. Job – Like Job, she comes to the end of herself and simply waits on the Lord, concluding that understanding the reason for pain and sorrow is beyond the scope of the human mind. "Where does wisdom come from? Where does understanding dwell? It is hidden from the eyes of every living thing…" *Job 28: 20, 21*

c. Jesus – Crying out, "My God, my God, why hast Thou forsaken me," she comes to the end of herself and surrenders her ego, her will, to her Lord.

Herein lies the secret to her victorious and peaceful death – she "died before she died."

"When you surrender to what is and so become fully present, the past ceases to have any power. The realm of Being, which had been obscured by the mind, then opens up. Suddenly a great stillness arises within you, an unfathomable sense of peace. And within that peace, there is joy. And, within the joy, there is love. And at the innermost core, there is the sacred, the immeasurable, that which cannot be named." *Practicing the Power of Now*, Eckhart Tolle

Author Madeleine L' Engle notes there is the slightest distinction between resignation and acceptance, yet the choice of one over the other makes all the difference in one's life and outlook. Resignation leads to hardness, while acceptance generates softness and gentleness; resignation builds crust, while acceptance leads to vulnerability; resignation leads away from God; acceptance brings one closer to Him. L'Engle, *Letters*

My mother offered no resistance to life. She did not have a hard crusty bone in her body. She was soft, gentle, vulnerable; Love personified.

Like a deep lake, she existed in a state of ease, lightness, and grace. On the surface, the water might be ruffled and rough, but underneath, at the level of Being, it was peaceful, still, undisturbed.

"Next to the might of God, the serene beauty of a holy life is the most powerful influence for good in the world." Dwight L. Moody

"Be still and know that I am God." *Psalm 46:10*

"He…in the long way I must trace alone
Will lead my steps aright."

Ruddy and his shebird home in Arctic mudflats

Barn and Silo, Schmidt Farm

Chapter 2

Country Dairy Past and Present

"And Ruth said, 'Entreat me not to leave thee, or to return from following after thee: for whither thou goest, I will go; and where thou lodgest, I will lodge: thy people shall be my people, and thy God my God: Where thou diest, will I die, and there will I be buried: the Lord do so to me, and more also, if ought but death part thee and me.'" *Ruth 1:16, 17*

"When Henry, ever the romantic, scooped up his petite bride, Ellen (all 5'4" and 90 pounds of her) carried her across the threshold, up the back stairway, and deposited her on the kitchen floor of their new home, their life together officially began. Their lives would be fashioned and shaped by the house on the hill, but, in turn, the farm would forever bear the stamp of their presence." *In the Garden*, pp. 14, 15

Country Dairy
Looking Back, Moving Forward
A Week With Hinie and Ellen
www.countrydairy.com

It's summertime and I'm at the family farm, Country Dairy, with my grand-boys. Country Dairy is their favorite place to visit. They drink bottomless cups

of chocolate milk, say hello to the cows munching grass in the pasture, search for a stray cat in the barn, and jump off hay bales like I did when I was their age, growing up on the farm. They're so familiar and comfortable here, you'd think they owned the place.

Filled with nostalgia, I walk the familiar haunts of my childhood. The dramatic changes the farm has undergone over the past years can't dim the memories.

The farm store, where we begin our visit, sits on the old asparagus field, where, long ago, I walked, with my siblings, snapping off tall green sturdy stalks and placing them in my basket. The cherry orchards are gone, but I remember standing on tippy-toes, atop a 10-foot ladder, stretching to pluck the cherries at the tops of the trees, placing them in my pail, affixed to me with a shoulder harness. The bean fields are no more, but I recall bending over the bushes and stripping them of their bounty. My father was usually around, if not physically harvesting the crop with us, then walking a row or two, offering encouragement, or bringing us a snack – usually Kool-Aid and a homemade cookie or piece of cake from my mom.

The garden is grassed over, but I envision my mother, Ellen, pulling up radishes and onions and tending her row of peonies. Her rose garden is gone, but I remember their fragrance, which filled the house when she brought them inside, called them by name, and lovingly arranged them in bouquets.

From the farm store, I look east, past the main barn, where the cows graze in the pasture and I imagine my father, Henry, guiding the plow as he walked back and forth across the field behind his workhorses, Maude and Daize. During hay harvesting season, we rode the wagon in from the fields.

I look up the hill, past the evergreen trees, where the cherry orchard once stood, and see my mother pinning the washing to the clothesline, hoping no cars would drive by to raise dust and undo her morning's toil.

I look across the highway to the west and think of my parents sitting on their front porch, "lifting their eyes to the hills." On a clear day, my father claimed he could see all the way to Lake Michigan. In the cool of the evening, after their chores were done, they retired to the porch, ending their day with a symphony of surround sound – the humming of the cicadas, the croaking of the frogs in the pond, the rising whistled call of the bob-white, the haunting cries of the Eastern whip-poor-will, singing its name, and sometimes from afar, the soft quavering whistles of an Eastern screech owl. My parents were at peace with each other and their Lord.

My grandfather, Andrew Van Gunst, was just a lad when he and his family sailed to this country from Friesland. When his parents and sibling died of consumption, shortly after arriving in the New World, Andrew went to live with an uncle on a nearby farm, earning his room and board as a farmhand. At 18 years of age, he purchased 40 acres and in 1901 he began farming the land that is now Country Dairy.

He worked the land for over 50 years, and in 1957 he sold the farm – by then 80 acres, to his son, Henry, my father. My brother, Wendell, purchased the farm in 1968 and transformed it into one of the top dairy operations in the country, with top-performing, prize-winning Holstein cattle. Wendell retired in December 2008 and passed the farm on to his children. Today, Country Dairy is a fourth-generation centennial touring farm. Take a tour of the farm and watch a video to learn the history of the farm in the Moo School. Afterward, visit the farm store/restaurant, where you can enjoy a meal, purchase milk and other dairy products, including homemade cheese, and top off your visit with rich creamy Country Dairy ice cream.

I wrote a memoir of my parents' life on the farm because I wanted my children, grandchildren, and visitors to the farm and farm store to appreciate the farm's legacy and history.

"Look, Grandma Jan, we found a cat!" Awakening from my reverie, I see my grandboys on top of a pile of hay bales, proudly hugging a tawny tom. Back to the present…

"The farm has changed since they lived here;
Country Dairy is now its name.
But the lessons earned from Hinie and Ellen
Hard work, diligence, and faith – are the same."
Country Dairy A Week with Hinie and Ellen, a pictorial memoir

Country Dairy: *Our Town* Revisited

The books in the Country Dairy series portray life in the 1930s, when my parents, Henry and Ellen Van Gunst, lived and worked on a small farm in west Michigan, the site of present-day Country Dairy.

The first book, *Country Dairy: A Week with Hinie and Ellen*, a memoir, describes a typical week on the farm and the chores that comprised a major part of my parents' lives:

"On Thursday, Ellen bakes her bread, mixing and kneading the dough. She places the loaves in waiting tins, then into the oven they go."

"Hinie leaves early to milk the cows. A frothy stream fills his pails. The cows low softly, waiting their turns, gently swishing their tails."

The second book, *In the Garden: An Ordinary Woman, An Extraordinary Life, A Memoir*, traces my mother's spiritual pilgrimage as a homemaker and a helpmeet for Henry, and like the pictorial memoir, describes the details involved with eking out a living on the farm within the larger story of her life.

"While guiding the plow in the fields behind the workhorses, Maude and Daize, Henry listened to the birds chirping and singing.…The hawks hovered high over the maple tree as he snapped the tall green spindly asparagus stalks. He rose with the sun {to milk the cows}, and watched it rise over the eastern hills, arc across the sky and plunge into the western horizon, an orange ball of fire, at day's end." *In the Garden*, pg. 35

"The variety of jobs facing Ellen was mind-boggling.…she needed to learn how to cook proper meals for a hard-working man like her Henry… breakfast, dinner, and supper with morning, afternoon, and evening snacks in between…" *In the Garden*, pg. 24

After writing the memoir, I decided to add a study guide to foster discussion of the many varied themes contained in the book.

One of the most important themes – the daily grind of everyday chores, triggered a memory of the play, *Our Town*, by Thorton Wilder. I had read and discussed the play for an English class in high school, but now I reread it with new meaning. Readers may wish to read/reread the play as well.

I was captivated by the many stark similarities between the lives of the characters described in Wilder's play and the lives of my parents:

Both take place in small towns, New Era and Grover's Corners; both focus primarily on two families, the VanGunsts and Postemas, the Webbs and Gibbs; both take place in the early/mid-1900s; both stress the everyday activities and routines of daily life; both involve tragedy/near-tragedy of childbirth; both describe the love between God and His created beings and the love between humans. But the most striking similarity was in the use of the term "extraordinary."

A summary of *Our Town* states: "…Wilder leaves us with a strong feeling that though mundane routines and events of our everyday lives may be repetitive, the details are what makes life interesting and deserving of our attention. Wilder's intent, in writing *Our Town*, was to make ordinary lives *extraordinary*." *Cliff Notes* (italics mine)

Voila! That was both my intention and my dilemma in describing the life of my mother:

"…I wanted to call the memoir, *In the Garden: My Mother – An Extraordinary Life*, because I truly believe she was extraordinary, but I didn't use the term because I sensed it would have made her feel uncomfortable. She never thought of herself as anything other than a humble ordinary woman of faith, who loved and served her Lord in the place where she felt called to serve; however, her life is a testimony to the power of God in the lives of ordinary people, who surrender to His will and become extraordinary. This use of the term, "extraordinary," describes my mother and in this context, I believe she would have approved its usage. *In the Garden*, pp. 138,139

Moo! Country Dairy Goes to Africa

November 2011. "Wendy, do you know a dairy farmer we could send to Uganda to look at a situation there?" the voice asked. "Well," replied my brother, "I know only one. That'd be me."

That phone conversation with Martin Mutuku was the beginning of Country Dairy's 9-yr. partnership with Partners Worldwide, an organization that connects professionals with people in similar businesses in developing countries.

Wendell Van Gunst was a perfect choice. Retired after 44 years as owner of Country Dairy (May 1964 - December 2008), a four-generation dairy farm in west Michigan, he was struggling. "I still love this business. What am I going to do?" He couldn't imagine a future without some kind of meaningful work.

When he accepted Mutuku's invitation to visit Uganda, he'd already made visits to India and Kenya. He was struck with the masses of people and debilitating poverty everywhere.

In his book, *A Path Marked Out, A Farm Boy's Journey to find God's Path*, Wendell chronicles the founding of Country Dairy, MI, Country Dairy, Gulu Uganda (CDGU), and the challenges faced along the way.

A CSGU Advisory board was formed and in February 2012 Wendell made his first trip to Uganda. What he found was a dairy industry that had collapsed during the reign of Idi Amin and 20 years of civil war under Joseph Kony and the Lord's Resistance Army, when soldiers kidnapped boys and conscripted them into the army. Often they would corral families into grass huts and order their sons to set the hut ablaze. He met Tonny, CDGU's future manager, who, with his brother, narrowly escaped a raid.

That August land was purchased and by July 2013, in less than one year, the barn and silo were finished and the first modern dairy set-up in Uganda was in place. The building site was leveled using a WWI bulldozer! Pouring the cement foundation was a community affair – all day long, women carried well water in jugs on their heads, others pounded rocks into little pieces, trucks unloaded piles of sand, and women, yes, women! hauled finished batches to the building site in wheelbarrows. The foundation had to fit exactly the steel frames being

shipped from America. When the containers arrived, the contents were so jumbled, Wendell likened sorting them out to doing a jigsaw puzzle. The different electrical current in Africa frequently burned up their tools. The bricks they made for the foundation of the bunker silo were so huge, they produced only two a day, 100 in two months.

Next was planting crops, so cattle could be purchased. Filling the stalls with cows was the most emotional moment for Wendell. By January 2018, they had 22 cows. The first milking called for a celebration!

A dairy processing plant from Israel was installed and in time a yogurt-making operation was added. Now half of the milk output goes into yogurt. Labeling, marketing, and distributing are challenging since there's no grocery system in Uganda.

From left: Martin Mutuku, Tonny Kidega, Wendell

Remembering how his dreams of owning a dairy farm came true with help from family and friends, Wendell was committed to helping others realize their dreams. In 2015, CDGU built a school, where aspiring farmers learn about modern dairy practices and watch them put into action in the barn.

CDGU has won national awards, hosted thousands of visitors, trained over 3000 dairy farmers/managers, and inspired hundreds of students on field trips. It currently employs fifty and has a staff of 20, representing 200 households. It's a pillar of the dairy industry not only in northern Uganda, but in entire East Africa, helping its people rise from the ashes of war, poverty, abduction, and massacre.

Wendell recalls the words on a plaque that hung on a wall in our home:

"Only one life will soon be past. Only what's done for Christ will last." He no longer has to wonder about what to do in retirement. God marked out his path.

Wendell, right, with his older brother Roger and their dog, Laddie

Juvenile Tri-colored Heron

Chapter 3
For the Birds

"A bird does not sing because it has an answer. It sings because it has a song." Chinese proverb

For the Birds – Count your Blessings: Count Things with Feathers!

This Christmas I'm adding something new to my holiday traditions. I'm participating in the National Audubon Society's Christmas Bird Count (CBC), held in mid/late December or early January and along with birders and bird lovers across the country, I'll head outdoors with binoculars, pad, and pencil to count birds!

Egret

Roseate Spoonbill

This annual event occurs in over 2000 "counts" in the United States. For over 100 years, Audubon Society members and friends have been counting birds, thereby helping ornithologists and environmental scientists understand bird population, habits, movements and contributing to the understanding of climate change. A recent "count" spotted the roseate spoonbill, native to southern climes, in northern Minnesota, where it's cold!!

Here's how the CBC works: Audubon members and friends are divided into geographical areas called "counts." Citizens within these local "counts" gather information on a designated day and submit it to their CBC coordinator, who in turn, gathers all the information from his/her count circle and enters it into the Cornell Lab of Ornithology. What I find amazing is that the objects of this gargantuan effort – the birds – are oblivious to it, going about their daily business of adding music, hope, and beauty to the world.

According to *Australian* legend, birds came to earth, when a rainbow shattered and its shards of color turned into birds as they fell: the glowing, jewel-like reds, greens, and blues of the hummingbirds; the bold red, white, and black of the woodpeckers; the blue of bluebirds and indigo buntings; the slash of red on the shoulders of red-winged blackbirds, and the full suit of red worn by male cardinals. *The Wonder of Birds*, Jim Robbins. Robbins's book changes the way we humans, perceive birds, moving them from the background of our lives to the foreground, from the quotidian to the miraculous.

In the Christmas Bird Count, we start by counting birds and hopefully move to a realization and appreciation of how much these fellow-travelers, on our planet, add to our lives – creatures who can fly halfway across the globe, nonstop dive ten times deeper into the ocean than a human, fly backward and upside down, and more things we cannot even imagine.

So, this year or next, count your blessings by counting birds! For more information: National Audubon Society –
https://www.audubon.org/conservation/science/christmas-bird-count.

Note The National Audubon Society developed from a grassroots campaign, in the late 1800s, to save the Great Egret, which was hunted to near extinction by the millinery industry for the long ostentatious feathers, called aigrettes, it grows during its breeding season.

Great White Egret Aigrette Feathers

Janet Hasselbring

Peacock Feather

Hope is a Thing with Feathers*

Feathers are one of nature's most exquisite and versatile designs. All birds – and *only* birds – have them.

I'm holding a peacock's feather as I write. It's a foot long, nearly weightless, and soft as silk. Feathers are dead. Like hair, they're made of keratin, one of nature's toughest proteins – sheer, light, and strong. My feather is durable enough to protect a bird – in this case, a peacock – fleeing through dense tangles of grass and brush.

Birds get a new set of feathers every year. If damaged they can shed them to make way for new growth. This peacock's loss was my gain.

Feathers evolved from the scales of dinosaurs, the first birds. But why? Did they arise for warmth? Or for show, to impress rivals or the opposite sex? For protection against parasites or predators? Paleontologists don't have a definite answer.

Whatever the reason, feathers are amazing. They are porous, made up of tiny microscopic air gaps. Huge volumes of air inside the feather are the secret to how precisely wing feathers keep birds in the air. Feathers act as a bird's GPS. Oddly enough they grow branched, like a tree.

If I haven't convinced you to nominate feathers for the 2019 "Seven Wonders of the World" list, consider this:

My peacock feather's gorgeous greens, brilliant blues, and loamy earth hues are the ultimate eye candy. Feathers have the most vibrant colors in the natural world, and while they're useful for sexual attraction and camouflage, their beauty led to the near extinction of many species of birds. For nearly three decades, starting in the 1870s, there was an enormous global craving for feathers to adorn women's hats. Snowy egrets were killed by the thousands for their brilliant white plumes and the long delicate trailing nuptial plumes, aigrettes, that grow off the backs of their heads during mating season. Their mass killings left the earth looking snowcovered. The grassroots campaign to end this savagery led to the formation of the National Audubon Society.

We use feathers to describe how light something is, e.g., "as light as a feather," but interestingly enough, the extreme lightness of a bird's feathers is more integral to sustained flight than its muscles.

Golden Eagle

The lightness and size of the golden eagle's feathers allow it to soar higher than any other bird. To the Native Americans, it's a "spirit bird," because it soars higher and can see and hunt better than any other, bridging heaven and earth.

"The golden eagle is our messenger to the Creator," notes Lee Plenty Wolf, a spiritual teacher in the Oglala Lakota tribe. Its feathers were, and still are, sacred, representing the highest values of trust, bravery, and honor.

I stroke my feather. It is exquisitely soft; in fact, feathers are the softest thing nature produces. We cram duck and goose down feathers into pillows, duvets, and mattresses because they make the warmest and lightest types of clothes and bedding. It's amazing how something nearly weightless is one of the most effective natural insulators known to us. Humans have never been able to replicate them.

The world's best-quality down is eiderdown, which comes from a wild sea duck, the common eider, whose feathers help it survive the harshness of the winter wind-whipped northern seas in the Arctic mudflats. Due to the eiderdown's rarity, superb quality, and labor-intensive gathering, an eiderdown comforter can range anywhere from $3,000 to $20,000.

Eiders

I lay my feather down and reflect on the spirit bird, soaring high, bringing messages to the Creator. I remember other sacred figures of speech that have brought comfort and hope to many a weary pilgrim: "He shall cover thee with His feathers and under His wings shalt thou trust." *Psalm 91:4* Again, "They that wait upon the Lord shall renew their strength; they shall mount up with wings as eagles…" *Isaiah 40:31*

Feathers. Birds – and *only* birds – have them.

*"Hope is a Thing With Feathers
That Perches in the Soul,
It sings the song without the words
And never stops at all.

And sweetest – in the Gale – is heard –
And sore must be the storm –
That could abash the little Bird
That kept so many warm –

I've heard it in the chillest land –
And on the strangest Sea –
Yet – never – in Extremity,
It asked a crumb – of me." Emily Dickinson

For a video showing the magnificent golden eagles visit https://www.youtube.com/watch?v=Sqzj4T7lVo8 or https://www.youtube.com/watch?v=azQJKhN1yNs

Hope Springs Eternal

10 Reasons to Hope

"Whenever you read these words, day or night, there are birds in the heavens of the Western Hemisphere, migrating" *Living on the Wind*, Weidensaul

Spring is in the air. As human snowbirds head home, their mass exodus is duplicated by millions of aerial fliers weaving an incredible tapestry across the heavens, traveling from as far south as Patagonia, north to the Arctic mudflats. While human snowbirds navigate with complex GPS systems, these avian flying machines' have navigational systems embedded in their brains.

They face incredible odds on their migratory flights: predators, storms, exhaustion, dehydration, satellite towers (over 75,000 of them!), windmills, and skyscrapers lit at night.

"Hope springs eternal," states Alexander Pope in his *Essay to Man*, whose dictum is as profound as it is poetic. Hope is the belief that in difficult circumstances things will get better. Hope is unique to our species because it requires words and thoughts to contemplate possible future events. While birds may sense impending events, such as crashing into a metal needle piercing the sky, they cannot conceptualize the future.

These feathered dynamos need hope, but according to Emily Dickinson, they also inspire hope with their amazing aerial feats:

"Hope is a thing with feathers,
That perches in the soul.
It sings the song without the words
And never stops at all." Dickinson

1. Blackpoll warbler – this little meatball, weighing 1/3 - 1/2 ounce (an empty pop can), and 4" long, skims wooded peaks, skirts urban skyscrapers, and crosses vast stretches of water, for 9000 miles, chasing summer.

2. Red Knot – also known as the Moonbird, because in its 20 years of flight, it will have flown the equivalent distance of to the moon and back.

3. White-rumped sandpiper – flies 9000 miles twice a year.

4. Arctic tern – weighing in at less than half a pound, it was for years the distance record-holder with its 44,000-mile yearly journey between the polar caps.

5. Shearwater – In fall 2006, a team of researchers outfitted sooty shearwaters in New Zealand with satellite tracking devices. Flying in a giant figure eight over the Pacific basin, they journeyed 39,000 miles a year. (These avian wonders can also dive up to 225 feet beneath the ocean's surface searching for squid.)

6. A female bar-tailed godwit flew 7,145 miles *nonstop* from Alaska to New Zealand. In nine days, she braved the waters of the vast Pacific, without a single meal, rest, or drink.

7. Golden Plover – not quite a foot long, weighing all of 6 ounces, this hardy bird flings itself into the air twice every year for a journey of nearly 20,000 miles. It can reach air speeds of 70 mph.

8. Black-bellied Dunlin – flying so tightly packed, they seem scarcely a wingspan apart, these birds wheel and turn in perfect synchronization, exhibiting a phenomenon known as cluster flocking.

9. Spectacled Eider – braving the winter gales and sub-zero temperatures of the Arctic tundra, eiders stay home, their bodies designed expressly for life in the frigid waters of the Arctic.

10. Ruddy turnstone – the dangers of migration are many and lethal: "The moon and stars are fading… when another enemy strikes – this one a killer. Out of the mist, a metal needle emerges. Ruddy veers to the left, missing the needle's fangs by a hair's breadth. Splat! The entire right wing of the flock crashes into the tower. They are killed instantly. The flock shudders, resets their position, and flies

on. The feathered remains of their fellows explode into the air and drift lazily to the ground." *Ruddy: Living on the Wind*, Hasselbring. And let's not forget Ruddy's shebird – leaving two weeks after Ruddy and the males, she hopes to meet up with her mate in the Arctic tundra, where they will nest and breed.

"Hope springs eternal in the human breast:
Man never is, but always to be blest:
The soul, uneasy and confin'd from home,
Rests and expatiates in a life to come." *An Essay to Man*, Pope

Baby Robins

I Have a Bird in Spring*

"But it is with poets…that birds achieve their most familiar and powerful poetic status as both symbols of imaginative freedom in their flight and substitutes for the poet in the full-throated ease of their singing." Introduction, *Bright Wings*, by Billy Collins

> "I have a bird in spring
> Which for myself doth sing –
> The spring decoys.
> And as the summer nears –
> And as the rose appears,
> Robin is gone." *I Have a Bird in Spring*, Emily Dickinson, Verse 1*

It's springtime in Michigan. My husband and I are back home after wintering in Florida. We decided years ago not to return home 'til we're sure spring has arrived. We go south to avoid winter; why deal with its vestiges upon our return? We've been "April fooled" on more than one occasion with random snow squalls, icy roads, and freezing temperatures. Now we play it safe and return in May.

We Michiganders have an unwritten rule that you can't officially announce the arrival of spring until you've seen your first robin bouncing sturdily across the lawn singing his cheery roundelay. Since robins' diets consist primarily of worms, they won't return north until the ground is thawed, which makes them such accurate predictors of spring. Unless they're "April fooled" of course. We often have snow in April – even then, if you spot a robin, it's spring. It doesn't matter the month or time of year.

This year robins heralded spring with a deposit of four bright sky-blue eggs in an old dilapidated nest, on the railing outside our porch. I was thrilled. Birding up close and personal!

For the next two weeks, the shebird and I had coffee hour together. I read my devotions and she sat faithfully on her nest. One day, instead of four eggs, I discovered a mass of feathers and gaping beaks. The chicks had arrived!

The feeding frenzy was on! As the parents swooped in with draggling worms, the chicks jostled about, jockeying for position. By now, I was more than a curious spectator; I felt like a doting godmother. As I watched the feeding ritual I noticed one large chick always forcing itself to the front of the line, its mouth  wide open in anticipation. A bully! This wasn't "The early bird gets the worm," it was "The largest mouth gets the worm." Did the parents have a system to make sure their chicks were being fed equally I wondered? Turns out, they didn't.

One day noticing only three gaping mouths, I looked closer and saw one chick lying on its back, motionless, its mouth closed. It wasn't Big Mouth.

During the incubating, hatching, and feeding, we kept up our normal activities, but nothing seemed to deter or distract the parents from feeding and guarding their chicks. Even Maggie, our curious Welsh terrier, who woofed and yapped at all the activity, didn't deter their parental responsibilities.

By now the three remaining chicks had gotten so big, they were spilling out of the nest. On the day I noticed only two chicks, I realized they were beginning to fledge. I panicked. I'd become attached to my little feathered friends. I didn't want them to leave, yet, being a writer, how could I begrudge them their "freedom of flight and full-throated ease of singing?"

And then there was one. I was determined to see this one leave if it took all day. And it nearly did. The last one took her own sweet time, but the drama was worth the wait:

The mother robin flits about below sweetly calling out encouragement.

"Cheer up, cheer up. Come on down."

Her chick perches on the edge of the nest.

"Hey Mom, it's kind of nice having all this room to myself."

"I know dearie, but you can't stay up there forever."

"Wow, it's a long way down there…"

"Cheer up. Cheer up," more seriously now. "You can do it."

"I'm scared."

"This is no time for hesitating my dear. There are some nice juicy worms down here but you're going to have to come and get them. One, two, three, GO!!"

The chick fluffs out her feathers, flaps her wings a few times, and then plumps back down in the nest.

Robin

"Cheer up. Cheer up," with a severe whistle, "Spread those wings and fly! You really must do this – now!"

"OK. I'm coming. Getting ready... Will you catch me if I fall?"

"I'm here. Got you covered, all the way."

With that the last chick spreads her wings and half flying, half plummeting, joins her mother. Together they fly into the woods. They're gone. It's quiet, eerily quiet. I feel bereft.

The next morning I head out to the porch with my coffee. Creature of habit, I glance at the railing, but the nest is empty. I feel a twinge of sadness knowing my bird odyssey is over.

And then I hear them – a string of clear rapid whistles from deep in the wood. "Cheerily, cheerily." My heart leaps with joy. My robins haven't left me after all.

"...Then will I not repine,
Knowing that Bird of mine –
Though flown –
Shall in a distant tree
Bright melody for me
Return." *I Have a Bird in Spring* by Emily Dickinson

Brown Pelican

Quirks

Quirks, defined by Webster, are peculiar behavioral habits. Now be honest. If someone is described as quirky, doesn't that conjure up flattering images to you? Not to my husband, Donald, it doesn't. He's a CPA, a financial wizard, who likes life neat and orderly, to which I respond, "How dull, how dreary, how public like a frog." He's not convinced. Good thing opposites attract.

One of my quirks, according to Donald, is my system of filing. My life is an accumulation and assortment of heaps and mounds. Filing cabinets are not useful to me. I like my stuff out in the open not stored away out of sight because out of sight is out of mind and if I can't see my stuff, I might forget about it. The thing is, I can always find what I'm looking for because I alphabetize the papers in my heaps. This irritates Donald no end.

Then there's the issue of time. He feels a need to be on time, but when we're scheduled to be somewhere, I get this energy burst (like the day I delivered my babies), and bustle about doing odd jobs around the house or running errands on the way. I think being on time, or God forbid, early, is a waste of time. Being fashionably late is my way. It's well... it's fashionable.

Another quirk – he could be nice and call it an interesting character trait – is how deftly I can flit from one topic of conversation to another. My children have more experience conversing with me and have learned to follow as I switch nimbly from one subject to another but my husband can't keep up and it rattles him.

It's funny how I know exactly where I am in our dialogue and he's hopelessly lost. I'm sure he could list more of my "interesting character traits," but you get the idea.

I was starting to get down on myself but then my husband retired and we began wintering in Florida. That's when I started watching birds. I'd never been especially interested in birds, but the wild/shorebirds and water-

Brown Pelican

fowl in Florida were so exotic, I began writing a series of children's books and magazine articles about them.

While doing research for my writing, I discovered many interesting facts about birds. I discovered they have quirks too. We're kindred spirits!

For example, in one of my books, *Presley's First Day of Fishing*, Presley, a fledgling brown pelly, puts a "quirky" little twist into his dive just before he hits the water to avoid committing a painful belly flop. How cool is that! In another tale, *Ossie the Brave Fish Hawk*, Ossie, an osprey, catches a fish and turns it around headfirst in his talons to make his flight home more aerodynamic. Quirky! Laughing gulls sit on pelicans' heads attempting to steal their fish and blue wing

Blue-Winged Teal

teals can spring into flight from a standstill. Birds, called dabblers upend with their tails in the air and nibble food off the bottom of a cove or pond. Anhingas and cormorants play hide-and-go-seek in the water, diving in one place and emerging minutes later, halfway across the cove. A Northern Mockingbird, can mimic any sound it hears, even an alarm clock!

One spring morning, while walking around Pelican Cove, our winter home, I notice a pair of Yellow-crowned Night Herons building a nest high up in the branches of a slash pine. As I watch, the male flies in with a twig in his mouth. He transfers it, ever so carefully, from his beak to the shebird's, whereupon she stuffs it into a heap – yes, a *heap* – of twigs that were the beginnings of a nest.

Yellow-Crowned Night Herons

Another thing I've noticed from my birdwatching is that birds flit about and they are very *busy* and *energetic*. I've pointed out these traits to Donald. He's not impressed.

No matter. I remind him that Welsh terriers are a rare breed and he needs to stop at the bank. Check it out, I say. *Check out what?* Welsh terriers! There are very few breeders in the country. Did you forget it's cleaning day tomorrow? What is your friend's name? *What friend?* You know the one who had shoulder surgery yesterday. I should send him a card. Now let's see, in which heap did I put his address?

Janet Hasselbring

Cardinals

Randomness and a Cardinal

A pair of Northern Cardinals have me seeing red this spring. Their constant flitting back and forth from the feeder makes me feel certain they've nested in my backyard. I envision the shebird building the nest while the male stays close, exuberant in song. As she incubates the eggs, I imagine the male bringing her food, their bills touching slightly as she accepts the seed. Together they'll work to exhaustion feeding their first brood of nestlings.

I awake to jubilant calls, "Cue, cue, cue," "Cheer, cheer, cheer," and "Purty, purty, purty," their countersinging – one trilling several phrases, which the other completes – beautifully expressing the harmony of their life.

Imagine my delight when I come across a poem lauding my colorful tenants:

"Not to conform to any other color
Is the secret of being colorful.
He shocks us when he flies
Like a red verb over the snow…" *The Cardinal*, Henry Carlile

The poem got me thinking. For all that fascinates us about birds – the free-throated ease of their singing, their freedom of flight, beautiful plumage, and amazing migratory feats, it's perhaps the fleeting random encounters we have with them that are the most startling, the most enlightening. The fact that I cannot will them into view; cannot time my casual observations of the garden with their flits to the feeder or swoops through the trees, makes me realize how special the random moments when our lives intersect.

Randomness is the state of lacking a pattern or principle of organization; unpredictability.

"…even the smallest of birds can disappear on a whim and a wing, and conversely to cross your path when you least expect it. The fascination and thrill o birdwatching, whether it's keeping a casual eye on your backyard visitors or trekking into the wild in search of rare species, is entirely based on the element of randomness, of knowing that what you seek may elude you, but that something equally astonishing will take its place." *The Aviary*, Matt Merritt

I'm reminded of a random encounter my mother had with birds. It was March 1936. My father, Henry, brought his bride, Ellen, a city girl, home from their honeymoon to the Wisconsin Dells, to his small family farm in west Michigan. In my memoir, I describe Ellen's first morning on the farm:

"The farm is bleak in March. A grim austere landscape greeted Ellen, in her new housedress and apron, as she entered the kitchen and set about fixing breakfast for Henry, who'd left early to do the milking.

Suddenly her excitement shifted to a twinge of uncertainty. She felt vulnerable, alone, and lost. What was she doing here anyway? She knew nothing of farm life or being a farmer's wife. Her comfortable leisurely life back home seemed far away indeed.

Female Cardinal

Suddenly a flash of red flew past the window. Ellen noticed a male cardinal perched on a limb, his shebird a few branches up. *A pair of cardinals*, she thought, *just like Henry and me*. The sight of them lifted her spirits. She loved Henry with all her heart. He was a farmer; she was his helpmeet, his farmwife.

Humming, Ellen started the coffee, set the sausages sizzling, and stirred the pancake batter. Henry would soon be home. He'd be hungry. She'd better get breakfast ready.

Ellen's life on the farm had begun." *In the Garden: Ellen, a Memoir*, pg. 14

That moment helped set the foundation for a lifetime of faith, hope, and prayer.

Emily Dickinson's poetic words describe birds as emblems for the quick, lively, ungraspable, and wild essence that distances nature from humans, providing moments of serendipity, good fortune, and coincidences (two {random} events occurring simultaneously):

"Hope is a thing with feathers
That perches in the soul.
It sings the song without the words
And never stops at all."

My mother's faith and hope in God gave a random encounter meaning, transformed it into a coincidence, and imbued it with spiritual significance. I choose to think it was a miracle.

> "There is more sweetness in a single strain
> That falleth from a wild bird's throat
> At *random* in the lonely forest depths,
> Than there's in all the songs that bards wrote…" *The Dew and the Bird,*
> Alexander Pope, italics mine

Six Little Ducks I Never Knew – A Lesson in Vulnerability

My Welsh terrier, Maggie May, noticed them first. As we left the house for our morning walk, she tugged on the leash, pulling me over to the shrub by the front door. She wriggled her nose into the hedge and out flapped a duck, squawking and honking. *Oh no.* I thought, *She wouldn't. Not here.*

Working hard to separate the dense foliage, I held Maggie back and peered inside. There they were – six pearly white eggs. How had the duck managed to burrow in, build a nest, and lay her eggs in this tight, confined space?

For weeks I'd watched a pair of mallards waddling about the neighborhood, the missus heavy with eggs. I assumed she was looking for a nesting site. It never occurred to me she would choose my shrub.

When Maggie and I returned from our walk, I checked the shrub again. Out she flapped. She was serious about this...

I texted my friends with a photo of the eggs. One replied, "She knows you love birds. You can be a godmother."

Really? Okay, I like birds. I find them interesting. I've written books about them; however, I know nothing – zilch, nil, zeeero, about ducks, but even a bird-brain knows that laying a clutch of eggs, in a shrub, outside the front entrance to a home, where there is a curious dog, is not a good choice. In plain English, Mrs. Mallard, you are vulnerable!

Brene' Brown, in her book, "*The Gifts of Imperfection*," notes that vulnerability involves risk, uncertainty, and emotional exposure. It requires showing up and being seen. Are you listening, Mrs. Mallard?

The idea of being a godmother was intriguing. I'm a godmother to a niece, so I know we're chosen by parents to take an interest in their child's upbringing and personal development; to take care of them should anything happen to the parents. Being a godmother to ducklings seemed a bit odd, yet, it was obvious Mrs. Mallard needed help. Even if her eggs survived the snakes, raccoons, deer, chipmunks, foxes, and bears (hopefully, I'm kidding about the bears), they'd have to deal with navigating a fair distance from the nest to the water, the constant activity in and out of the house, and Maggie, an inquisitive terrier with a keen sense of smell. How would she have the uninterrupted time, a month, necessary to incubate and hatch her eggs?

I remember lyrics to a song I once sang to my children: "Six little ducks that I once knew; fat ones, skinny ones, pretty ones too…"

My interest growing, I put McCloskey's book, *Make Way for Ducklings*, on hold at the local library and begin researching ducks. Here's some of what I learn: Ducks close one eye in order to put half their brain to sleep while keeping the other eye and half of their brain awake and alert. Ducks have a remarkable degree of abstract intelligence. The female sits very tightly on her nest, her brown plumage blending in perfectly with the surroundings. Interesting, but would any of this help Mrs. Mallard?

A couple of days go by. Stealthy as thieves, Maggie and I come and go. Except for walks, I keep her inside.

One morning we sneak out for a walk. I glance at the shrub, envisioning Mrs. Mallard tucked tightly inside, ever the faithful mom sitting on her eggs. But, alas! There beside the shrub, is a scattering of eggshells. Not wanting to disturb the crime scene, I carefully peer inside. Shells everywhere. Not one egg is intact. A couple of cigarette butts nearby are a dead giveaway – the raccoons are the villains!

"Six little ducks I'll never know…" I recall my miscarriage and wonder if Mrs. Mallard feels the same excruciating sadness and grief I felt at the loss of a life never realized.

From my research, I'd learned that ducks feel loneliness, isolation, and grief much like humans, and since the male's role is over once the clutch is laid (he remains sexually potent for a while in case a replacement clutch is needed, but gradually loses interest and joins other males to molt), Mrs. Mallard would bear her loss alone.

Later that week, I see her across the driveway. I stay inside, respecting her need to inspect her nest and grieve her loss. Hours later, when I peek inside, she flies off for the last time. She'd been sitting for hours on a pile of eggshells. It breaks my heart.

Brown notes that one's inability to lean into the discomfort of vulnerability limits the fullness of important experiences, such as uncertainly, love, belonging, trust, joy, and creativity, but Mrs. Mallard knows this. She'll "rise strong" I know.

This fall a hunter will raise a rifle and take aim at a flock of ducks. Mrs. Mallard could be among them because she's my hero – she shows up and is seen. She's vulnerable, but whether she's brought down by a bullet or lives to lay another clutch of eggs, she'll always have a place in my heart.

About Brene' Brown

Brené Brown is a research professor at the University of Houston, best-known for her famous TED talk, "The Power of Vulnerability."

Brown has spent nearly two decades studying courage, vulnerability, shame, and empathy. All of her groundbreaking findings were included in five books that have easily become #1 *New York Times* bestsellers: *The Gifts of Imperfection, Daring Greatly, Rising Strong, Braving the Wilderness*, and *Dare to Lead*.

"The Power of Vulnerability" is about expanding perception and embracing our imperfections. Brown's's approach on how to cultivate courage, compassion, and connection turned a data presentation into one of the top five most-viewed TED talks of all time.

Brown has received numerous teaching awards including the Graduate College of Social Work's Outstanding Faculty Award. She is also the first person to have a filmed talk available on Netflix: *The Call to Courage*.

Due to her research, Brown has become an inspiration for millions of people around the world.

Roseate Spoonbill

Chapter 4
Bird Poems

"Writing free verse is like playing tennis with the nets down." Robert Frost

As a tennis junkie, I love this quote. In this chapter, I'm putting the nets up to write poems. To me, writing poetry is the ultimate short story and the finest example of omitting useless words.

"I wish our clever young poets would remember my homely definitions of prose and poetry; Prose is words in their best order; poetry is the best words in the best order." Coleridge

Janet Hasselbring

White Pelicans

An Invitation

Come along readers, come along with me
To a paradise – oh the things you'll see!

A veritable feast of spectacular sights
In water and air, on land, such delights.

(In water)
Ducks, herons, white pelicans by the herd.
The anhinga slimmed down to a sleek "snakebird."

(In air)
Overhead a kite, an eagle, an osprey,
The sharp-shinned hawk with a flash of blue-gray.

Bald Eagle

(On land)
White egrets and wood storks stalking about,
Wading and searching for fish to spear, no doubt.

These are just a few of the sights you'll see
So come, come along to Pelican Cove with me.

Wood Stork

You Birdbrain

When I use a certain word, my mom's face turns chalky-
white.
She says that to call someone stupid is rude and impolite.

So I've discovered another word that nicely fills the bill.
Now when someone does something stu…, well, I'll use
this word, I will.

Brown Pelican

When Johnny undoes his pen and spills ink all over his pants,
I'll call him a birdbrain, no matter what the circumstance.

And when Sally leaves muddy footprints all over the kitchen floor,
I'll say, "What are you doing, you birdbrain? Leave your shoes at the door!"

Then there's Bert, who climbed a tree and got his pants caught on a limb.
"Hey, birdbrain!" I call, "How's it going? Life looking a bit grim?"

"Oh no, Susie, didn't you read the sign, WET PAINT?
You're a birdbrain. When Mom sees what you've done, she's going to faint!"

Joey thought he was cute and stuck gum under his seat.
"You birdbrain, Joey. Someone finds this and you're a piece of dead meat."

I wonder if birds mind us taking their names in vain,
To describe stu… well, things kids do that are so very very lame?

How do you suppose the word, "birdbrain" first came into our vocabulary?
Was the first "ink-spiller" or "tracker-inner" a yellow-fronted canary?

Janet Hasselbring

Ibis

Bird Chat

Calling all *birds of a feather:* Come together!
It's time we had a chat.
It seems birds' names are being taken in vain!
We need to do something about that.

A bird in the hand is worth two in the bush.
Now what is the meaning of that?
Could it mean, *Don't count your chickens before they hatch,*
Or make sure before tossing high your hat?

Try to *kill two birds with one stone.*
Eek! Crak! That's scary! It makes me shiver!
Wait! Perhaps this means
It's best to be clever with only one arrow in your quiver.

If your friend is bald and lost his hair
Is it nice to say *He's bald as a coot?*
Your friend should just *stick his head in the sand,*
He shouldn't even *give a hoot!*

The early birds are *up with the larks*
They're *crowing about it* too.
Their prize for getting up early *is a worm*
Do you think that's worth getting up early for – now do you?

Lame ducks stay around too long
And it's dangerous for a duck just to sit.
During hunting season, if a duck's not in flight,
He's a *sitting duck* – an easy target for a hunter to hit.

If you strut around *naked as a jaybird*,
You'd be silly, *silly as a goose!*
This little incident could be your *swan song*,
It could hang around your neck like an *albatroose.*

If you're a *fly by night*,
You're here today and gone tomorrow.
Face it, my friend, you're just a flake
Not a Gibraltar or Kilimanjaro.

A *stool pigeon* has secrets no one else knows
He keeps his *pecker up*, they say.
He knows who has *flown the coop*
And why the *"chicken crossed the r…. {highway}."*

If you know *which comes first, the chicken or the egg*
Like an owl, you'd be wise.
A fledgling *not yet out of his pinfeathers*
Wouldn't have a clue about this, I surmise.

So *which came first the chicken or the egg?*
It's a question for eternity.
Socrates, eat your heart out.
It seems that birds, not you, invented philosophy!

They say that *going out on a limb* is taking a chance.
They can't be talking about the lark out there "atrillin."
They must mean the vulture, with *eyes like an eagle,*
Waiting out there for the killin'.

It's not nice, but you're called a *birdbrain*
For doing idiotic, stupid, silly stuff.
Acting cuckoo or *running around like a chicken*
With her… Hey, stop! Now that's enough!"

Knowing how to *feather your nest,*
Gives you *something to crow about.*
And if you don't put *all your eggs in one basket,*
You can be *proud as a peacock* – just shout it out!

So, my fine-feathered friends, never mind what they say.
When they *parrot* unkind and hurtful words.
Don't get *pigeonholed* or *all cooped up*.
Trust me, this talk is just *for the birds!*

Crows

Caw! Caw! Caw!

There are birds in my woods that continually squawk.
They'll mob a bald eagle, a great horned owl, and a hawk.
Caw, Caw, Caw! Caw, Caw, Caw!
Wanna bet their squawking gets them in trouble with the law?

The he-birds, she-birds, sisters, and brothers,
Take turns doing sentry duty – spying – for each other.
Caw, Caw, Caw! Caw, Caw, Caw!
To whom do you suppose they report what they saw?

These birds eat insects, grain, mice, and eggs.
With this diet, the question an answer begs,
Caw, Caw, Caw! Caw, Caw, Caw!
Do they cook or eat all of their food raw?

They're some of the most widely distributed birds.
They can be found all over the world in herds.
Caw, Caw, Caw! Caw, Caw, Caw!
They're even found in Little Rock, Arkansas!

Their bills are long, heavy, and tough as nails
In flight, they sport fan-shaped tails.
Caw, Caw, Caw! Caw, Caw, Caw!
They're pitch black right down to their paws!

You might mistake this bird for another
One that's alike in some ways but different in others.
One that's larger and has a different tail shape – a bird of lore,
Caw, Caw, Caw? "Quoth the raven, 'Nevermore!'"

So, we've identified you as a plain ordinary blackbird
And while I'll defend you against allegations that are absurd,
Be warned. I can't protect you from them enacting a law
Making it a crime for you to Caw, Caw, Caw!

Caw, Caw, Caw! Caw, Caw, Caw!
There you go again. If you're smart enough to draw.
If you can count, remember things, and solve a puzzle,
You should be smart enough to quiet down, so you don't end up wearing
a muzzle!

American Crow

Dabble, Dabbling, Diving Ducks

Dabble, dabbling, diving duck,
What are you doing with your head in the muck?
Dabble, dabbling, diving duck
It's yucky down there, Yuck, Yuck, Yuck YUCK!

Dabblers are very interesting birds.
Their eating habits are really quite rare.
If their food's on the surface they'll gobble it up,
If not, they'll upend with their tails in the air!

Dabble, Dabbling, Diving Duck,
What are you doing with your head in the muck?
Dabble, Dabbling, Diving Duck,
It's yucky down there, Yuck, Yuck, Yuck, YUCK!

The blue-winged teal has patches of blue.
On his head are crescents of white.
He doesn't need a running start to take off.
He can spring instantly into flight!

Blue-Winged Teal

The smallest dabbler is the green-winged teal.
A high flier, quick-moving and agile.
If he can't find his food on the surface,
He'll filter it from the bottom with his bill.

Dabble, Dabbling, Diving Duck,
What are you doing with your head in the muck?
Dabble, Dabbling, Diving Duck,
It's yucky down there, Yuck, Yuck, Yuck, YUCK!

The mallard is a dabbler with a bright green head.
The ground is his place of breeding.
If he's not *on* the water or dabbling *underneath*
He's probably in someone's yard "a'feeding."

The wood duck has glossy green feathers.
He likes to perch up in the trees.
So if he's not dabbling about in the water,
He's likely up high enjoying the breeze.

Dabble, dabbling, diving duck,
What are you doing with your head in the muck?
Dabble, dabbling, diving, duck,
It's yucky down there, Yuck, Yuck, Yuck, YUCK!

Sea ducks don't just put their heads under water,
They dive to the bottom of ponds.
These Olympian wonders dive down to 180 feet
Past Monet's water lilies and the Green Giant's fronds.

The merganser is a sea duck bold and daring.
He sports an extraordinary crested hood,
In the cavities of trees, you'll find his nest,
A safe place to raise his brood.

Hooded Merganser

Now ducklings are quickly on their own.
They leave home when they're only a day old.
Not only are they born knowing how to swim,
They leave the nest with just one leap, brash and bold.

Dabble, Dabbling, Diving Duck,
What are you doing with your head in the muck?
Dabble, Dabbling, Diving Duck,
It's yucky down there, Yuck, Yuck, Yuck, YUCK!

Note: Ducks are classified according to how they feed – Dabblers, Divers, and
Sea ducks

Flip, Flip, Flip It High

Have you met the Ruddy Turnstone,
With his long slightly upturned bill?
He feeds by flipping shells and stones,
Finding what he will.

Ruddy Turnstone

Mr. Ruddy Turnstone,
Would you flip a stone for me?
Let's find out what's underneath.
Let's see what we can see.

Flip, flip, flip it high,
In all kinds of weather.
Flip, flip, flip it high,
Here's a tiny feather.

Flip, flip, flip it high,
Blow the horn, sound the bell.
Flip, flip, flip it high.
Here's a shiny sparkling shell.

Flip, flip, flip it high.
Something soft and squiggly.
Flip, flip, flip it high.
A caterpillar, warm and wiggly.

Flip, flip, flip it high,
I see something not very big.
Flip, flip, flip it high.
Look, a teeny, tiny twig.

That's enough Ruddy Turnstone.
You can be on your way.
Go find yourself a worm or grub
Under a stone by the bay.

Janet Hasselbring

Yellow-Crowned Night Heron

Mrs. Yellow Crowned Night Heron

Hey, Mrs. Night Heron with the yellow-crowned crest,
High up in a slash pine, sitting on your nest.
How many chicks do you think there'll be –
As many as four or five or as few as three?

Settle in because you'll be up there for three weeks.
That's how long it'll be before you see baby beaks.
If you get tired of sitting, call on your trusty mate.
The mister can take a turn; males can help incubate.

If it should rain and you get soaked clear through,
I know you'll stay – leaving your nest is something you'd never do!
And if the wind should blow and buffet you about,
You'll hang on and hang in there I have no doubt!

Finally comes the day you've been waiting for –
Cracks appear, then more and more and more!
The eggs break, little gray balls roll out,
Soon your fuzzy little chicks will be running all about.

Brown Pelican

Pell-Mell Pelly

Hey you with the long bill and giant webbed feet
Hanging out by the cove, waiting for fish to eat,
You've come from Louisiana, the "Pelican State,"
Welcome to Florida and welcome to your mate.

I've been wondering about your large lower bill.
Is that pouch balloon useful or is it just a frill?
"A frill? No, no, no, no! But decide for yourself.
Watch me fish and you'll see my bill is a huge help.

Here I go flap, flap, flapping up high,
Spotting fish from up here takes a very good eye.
Check out my cool dive-bombing moves.
That's me splish-splooshing through the grooves.

Pelican

Watch me open my pouch balloon, as I snatch the fish I've caught.
This fish was a goner from the start, there's no doubt.
I drain off the water, tilting my long bill downward.
I'm ready to swallow my catch – am I not a clever bird?"

Watch out Mr. Pelly, a suspicious bird is flying near!
On no! He's landed on your head. He's acting very queer.
Shall I call for help? On your head is perched a thief,
Just waiting to snatch your catch! Oh my! Good grief!

"Don't worry, laughing gulls do this all the time.
Wouldn't you think that stealing fish would be a crime?"
Ha! Ha! Ha! Ha! Ha! Ha! "Do you hear that cackling?
It's shameful – stealing while they're laughing!"

Then, quick as a flash, my friend, Mr. Pelly
Tossed that fish down his throat to his belly.
"I learned how to do that in fishing school.
Isn't it remarkable? Isn't it just too cool?

So, now that you've seen my bill in action,
I'm assuming you have a favorable reaction.
You've seen my special gular pouch,
And I'm ready for an afternoon nap on the couch!"

And with that, Mr. Pelly flapped away
Off to his home along the shore by the bay.
I'm sure you'll agree after everything you've heard
Mr. Pell-Mell Pelly is quite a spectacular bird!

Copyright Lawrence M. Monat

Muscovy Duck

The Red-Faced Muscovy Duck

Why the red face, Mr. Muscovy Duck?
Are you embarrassed because of the many droppings (YUCK)
You've left by park benches and sidewalks everywhere?
Why don't you pick up after yourself? Why don't you care?

Pardon me, you're not embarrassed – is that what you said?
Then why, tell me why, is your face turning red?
Pardon me? You were born with that red splotch on your face?
Do you say it's part of the Muscovy Duck race?

You're a bulky blackish duck, that much I know.
You have special white patches on your wings, you're not status quo.
You've got a red un-feathered patch of skin from your bill to your eye…
I wondered why you seemed embarrassed and now I know why.

So I'm sorry about what I said to you before.
Here's a piece of advice while you're showing me the door.
When you're out by the park benches and the sidewalks everywhere
Clean up after yourself. Learn to care, care, care!

Janet Hasselbring

Roseate Spoonbill

The Roseate Spoonbill

Does the spoonbill eat his fish with a spoon?
And the crayfish he catches on a Sunday in June?

If he were a forkbill, he'd eat with a fork.
He'd have a sizzler or a grilled loin of pork.

A roseate knifebill would eat with a knife.
He'd cut up that sizzler to share with his wife.

But instead, our friend has a spatulate bill.
He can flip pancakes or snag burgers from the grill.

And get this – because his bill is spatulate
He'll never ever have a need for bait.

If that's not special enough, his bill swings to and fro.
This bill, most definitely, is not your status quo!

A swinging, sweeping, stupendous bill
One that's extremely useful; it's certainly not a frill!

There's nothing like it anywhere
And that my pink-feathered friend – that makes you rare!

Limpkin

Stop the Krr-owws Now!

Krr-oww! Krr-oww! Krr-oww!
It's the sound of the limpkin brood!
Poking about in mud and water
Searching for limpkin food.

Krr-oww! Krr-oww! Krr-oww!
It's the limping limpkin birds.
In the evening when all is quiet
Their piercing calls can be heard.

Krr-oww! Krr-oww! Krr-oww!
Wherever you nest; on the ground, in a tree.
Please, please, dear limpkin friends,
Please don't come nesting by me!

Krr-oww! Krr-oww! Krr-oww!
Ouch! These krowws are hurting my ears.
I don't mean to be rude,
But your krowws have brought me to tears.

Krr-oww! Krr-oww! Krr-oww!
This constant noise has made me a nag.
If you must continue this krowwing,
Would you consider wearing a muzzle or gag?

Krr-oww! Krr-oww! Krr-oww!
What's that? News too good to be true!
The limpkin brood has been invited
To live at the Limpkinville Zoo!

Krr-oww! Krr-oww! Krr-oww!

Great Horned Owl from
Ossie the Brave Fish Hawk

Chapter 5

Tales from Pelican Cove –
The Stories behind the Stories

"Always be a poet, even in prose." Charles Baudelaire

Writing poetry has helped me write better short stories, by limiting words and omitting useless words – hopefully, "trying to be poetic in prose by using and putting not only words in their best order, but the best words in the best order," has made my short stories more appealing and stimulating.

The books in the *Tales from Pelican Cove* series portray the wild/shorebirds of Florida and beyond – birds I observed on a small cove, surrounded by mangroves in Sarasota Bay, during the years my husband, Don, and I wintered in Sarasota, Florida.

The stories were inspired by the experiences I had with these amazing birds. Here are the stories behind the stories:

Book One – *Andy Discovers Peanut Butter and Discovers a New Friend*

Before wintering in Florida, I was pretty much oblivious to birds. I noticed them, but only in a cursory way. Birds were plentiful on the farm, where I grew up, and my parents were bird lovers. My father spent much of his time outside; the birds kept him company as he mended fences, pruned apple trees, or walked behind the horses guiding the plow back and forth across the fields. He knew birds by their songs as well as their colorful feathered coats. My mother's favorite was the chickadee, but alas she could never lure the plump little "dees" to nest near the house. At night, sitting on the porch after a busy day of chores, my parents listened to the whip-or-wills, the night owls, and the bob-whites.

Florida birds were different. From my first day at the cove, they demanded (and got) my attention. Comical brown pelicans dive-bomb the cove from dizzying heights, double-crested cormorants, play hide-and-go-seek – diving deep in one place only to resurface yards away, dabblers, such as the blue-winged teal, upend in the water, and great white egrets grace the sky, croaking "Cuk-cuk-cuk. Cuk-cuk-cuk." An egret lands on the mangroves with a fish in her sharply pointed bill. I watch fascinated as she throws the fish down her long slender throat, twisting and turning as she forces it into her stomach. Great "blues" (herons) stalk the shoreline foraging for food. One heron is so tame he never moves as my dog, Max, and I walk by him on the shell path surrounding the cove. Residents call him Bubba. They've tamed him with peanut butter.

Bubba was the seed for my first story, though the story would need more time and information to germinate. That came when I spotted the anhinga, a bird I had never heard of and certainly had never seen before. Sarasota is as far north as anhingas venture and they don't migrate. Conveniently, the anhinga chose the branch in front of our condo for its perch that first winter, so I had plenty of opportunities to watch him up close and personal.

Anhinga

In the water the anhinga resembles a sleek snakebird, diving deep in one place and resurfacing yards away, like the cormorant. But drying off on his perch, his oversized feathers are streaked and spotted with silvery-white. In the sun they glow with a greenish sheen.

One day I hear a ruckus at the branch. A great blue heron (Bubba?) has usurped the anhinga's perch, forcing him into the water. They seem to be having a friendly conversation. What is going on? With Bubba, the great blue, the anhinga, I name Andy, peanut butter, and a dash of imagination, I just may have the ingredients for a story:

"And that was how it happened. Every night, just before sundown, Bubba, the great blue heron, could be seen sitting on the branch overlooking the cove, with Andy, the anhinga, hovering nearby, fanning him with his large beautiful wings. When Bubba flies home, Andy resumes his rightful place on the branch and enjoys an evening snack of peanut butter!!" *Andy Discovers Peanut Butter*, pg. 17

Great Blue Heron

Note I: After *Andy* was published, I approached the local Audubon society about promoting my book. After reading it, they vociferously declined, explaining that they couldn't promote a book whose plot included feeding peanut butter to a wild bird, even though I explained the story was based on real-life experiences. At their suggestion, I added a caveat stating that feeding human food to wild birds is dangerous because the preservatives and food coloring it contains are harmful to their delicate digestive systems. This statement not only makes my book acceptable to birding and nature groups, but it gives me a platform for discussing this important issue with my readers as well.

Note II: Imagine my reaction when on an Audubon birding tour later that same year, the guide handed out little tubs of peanut butter, promising it would attract scrub jays, the birds we were seeking. Sure enough, in minutes I had a scrub jay sitting on my head!

Book Two – *What Do You See, Mrs. Night Heron?*

Mrs. Heron is sitting on her nest. While she waits for her eggs to hatch, she's entertained by the plentiful wild-life at the cove.

Like all the books in the *Tales* series, *What Do You See, Mrs. Night Heron?* is based on my experiences at the cove. That spring, I'd watched the yellow-crowned night herons building their nest in a slash pine tree.

Yellow-Crowned Night Herons

One morning I watch, fascinated, as the male heron flies in with a twig in his beak. He hands it off to his shebird, who pokes it down into the nest, while a third male, a sentry, watches from atop a neighboring tree.

Knowing it will take Mrs. Heron three to four weeks to incubate her eggs and wanting to incorporate as many birds as possible into my story, having the birds serve as entertainment for Mrs. Heron becomes the theme and storyline for the book.

What I couldn't have known when I was choosing birds to include in the story, was that my research would introduce me to the interesting world of bird piracy, lead to my third and fourth books, and provide inspiration for my seventh book.

Mrs. Heron sits on her nest. There is so much to see; time is flying by:

> "High above the cove, an osprey is soaring
> With his sharp striped eyes, he's on the move exploring.
> When he spies his prey, he plunges feet first,
> Then with a fish in his talons, he's off in a burst." *Mrs. Heron*, pg. 12

Osprey

Book Three – *Ossie the Brave Fish Hawk,*
showcases Ossie, an osprey, a bald eagle, named Baldwin, and a third raptor, a great horned owl.

Bald Eagle

"The bald eagle is certainly a sight to behold.
His stick nest is found high up in a tree fold.
From her perch, Mrs. Heron watches him at play
As he chases ospreys, trying to steal their prey."
Mrs. Heron, pg. 21

My research reveals that not only does the eagle steal from the osprey (which I already know), but that great horned owls are also pirates. They lay their eggs early in the winter, then attempt to steal an osprey's or eagle's nest in which to raise their young.

I'm careful to base my stories on facts, making them credible for my readers – not only for children, but also for recreational birdwatchers, and more serious birders, such as Audubon members.

Sometimes my research takes me "out on a limb," placing me in situations, where, to uphold the credibility of my books, I need to defend the facts I've included.

After Ossie was published, I was discussing the book with the director of an owl rescue center in Michigan. When I described the owl's attempt to steal Baldwin's nest, she took umbrage with the story, claiming that a great horned owl would never take on a ferocious bird such as an eagle. She seemed upset that one of her rescues, an owl, was being accused of piracy. I was taken aback, for if she was right, my book was not credible, so I did further research and found examples to back up my story.

That winter, back in Florida, I was sharing the book with members of an Audubon society. When I read the part of the story describing the owl's attempt to steal Baldwin's nest, I relayed my conversation with the rescue director in Michigan.

Suddenly a member of the audience stood. "Hold it right there," he interrupted, "please everyone, come with me." We followed him outside, where he pointed to a nearby tree. "See that eagle's nest?" he asked. "What is the bird sitting on the edge of the nest?" There it was. I wanted to jump for joy. Perched on the edge of the eagle's nest was a fledgling horned owl!

Note – the osprey is the only raptor that dives into the water feet first. And sometimes, when attacked by eagles, they fight back!

Copyright Lawrence M. Monat

Osprey & Bald Eagle

Book Four – *Presley's First Day of Fishing*

"The brown pelican swoops in to eat his fill.
His pouch hangs down from a large lower bill.
Above him, the laughing gull flies about
Hoping to snatch a stray mullet or trout."
Mrs. Heron, pg. 22

Aha! Another pirate on the loose. The brown pelican has always fascinated me with its kamikaze-style headfirst dives, its comical pouch balloon, and its ability to make fishing look easy. I've noticed that whenever pelicans are around, there are usually laughing gulls flying overhead. Now I know why. The gulls are attempting to steal the pelicans' fish!

Brown Pelican

Pelicans make fishing look easy, but it's complicated. The six-step process requires diving (from 60 or 70 feet up), scooping (up the fish), draining (off the water gulped in with the fish), pointing (the long bill upward), catching (in the throat), and finally swallowing (and securing) the fish. It's at the point of catching that the laughing gull tries to snatch the fish out of the pelly's bill – what Leonard, the gull in my story, does with Presley, the fledging brown pelican, out on his first solo fishing trip.

"Ha, ha, ha! Ha, ha, ha!" cackles Leonard from atop Presley's head. Presley doesn't think it's funny:

"Presley was smart enough to know he was in a tough spot. A thief was on his head and he would have to use his head to get him off." *Presley's First Day of Fishing*, pg. 12

Though Leonard steals his fish, the two become friends, and Presley ends up catching fish for Leonard and his family, becoming an expert in the process.

"Presley beat his wings in farewell and flapped away. He was beat tired but he had never felt so happy and proud. As he soared home, Leonard's peals of laughter followed him, echoing around and around the cove. His first day of fishing had been quite a day." *Presley's First Day of Fishing*, pg. 20

Laughing Gull

Book Five – *Mimi the Mimic and the Great Migration*

"At whatever moment you read these words, day or night, there are birds aloft in the skies of the Western Hemisphere, migrating." *Living on the Wind*, Scott Weidensaul

These words will always be special to me because they inspired Mimi, a story which portrays the annual migration of the great white pelicans from their winter feeding grounds in Florida to the Mississippi River Valley, the first stop on their way north for the summer – a story which didn't come easily to the pen.

It's winter 2014 at Pelican Cove. A year earlier I'd published my fourth book, *Presley's First Day of Fishing*, but now the well was dry. I was a writer without a story, and like an osprey without a fish, a night heron without a crab, or a limpkin without an apple snail, I was hungry for a story idea.

I know enough about writing to know that you can't force an idea, so I accepted my situation and resolved to enjoy the birds at the cove without feeling a compulsion to write about them.

Northern Mockingbird

One bird, in particular, the northern mockingbird, captured my attention that winter. She woke me up every morning. At first, I thought many birds were singing outside my window, but then I remembered the mockingbird's ability to mimic anything it hears, e.g. the ring of a cell phone, an alarm clock, a baby's cry, and other birds' songs and calls. Some mockingbirds have hundreds of bird calls in their repertoire.

Another bird that forced my attention was the white pelican, the original snowbird. The pelicans were so abundant, it was hard to ignore them. With ten-foot wingspans, they glide gracefully through the air. In the water, unlike their cousins, the brown pelicans, who dive for fish, the white pelicans herd them. They paddle about bringing the fish to the surface with their webbed feet and then scoop them up with their long flat orange bills. Being a snowbird myself, I was interested to learn more about them and their behavioral and migratory habits.

White Pelicans

Was it a coincidence these two birds caught my attention? Was there a story here? I've always believed that naming the characters in a story is important, for once they have a name, they come alive and help tell their own story, so I named the mockingbird Mimi and though she trilled out daily encouragement – her "Chack, chack, chacks," sounding like "Write, write, writes," I was in a thick fog as to how to put these two birds together in a story. I needed a theme, a plot.

Into the fog came my son and his family for a visit. One evening, while reading a book of Emily Dickinson's poems with my grandsons, we come across her poem, "Hope is a Thing with Feathers:"

> "Hope is a thing with feathers
> That perches in the soul.
> It sings the song without the words
> And never stops at all."

Voila! The fog cleared! I decided that hope would be the theme of my story and immediately the characters, the plot, and the action came together.

Mimi's story will always be special to me because it shows the important role birds play in our lives as symbols of hope.

I delved into the research on mockingbirds, white pelicans, the birds, which would be minor characters in the story, and migration. I began weaving the interesting facts I learned into the storyline:

"One day, returning to her nest in the mangroves, Mimi spots white pelicans swimming in the cove below. Their unusual frenetic activity puts her on full alert. *It's time*, she realizes.

What had looked to Mimi like chunks of ice and patches of lilies, were, in fact, her friends, the white pelicans. There were hundreds of them. They were herding and corralling fish into their throat pouches with their long flat orange bills." *Mimi*, pg. 7

Fact: Before takeoff, migratory birds gorge on food, which provides them with the necessary energy for their long arduous flights.

Mimi spends the rest of the day visiting her friends who live around the cove. Mimicking their calls, she entices them up close so she can relay her urgent message, *It's time*. She invites them to the cove the following evening. "Be there," she advises.

"...as the sun made its way across the sky and the late afternoon shadows appeared, the pelicans began swarming into the cove." *Mimi*, pg. 17

Fact: Migratory birds fly at nighttime because night air is less turbulent and they don't waste energy battling winds and contrary currents. They are also less exposed to danger from both hawks, which are exclusively diurnal flyers, and owls, which fly at night, may attack and do harm but aren't agile enough to actually take a bird out of the air.

The next afternoon Mimi's friends join her at the cove to bid farewell to the white pelicans who are departing on the first leg of their migratory journey. As the birds lift their giant black-tipped wings and take to the sky, the birds call out their farewells. Mimi sings:

"Chack, chack, chack. Chack, chack, chack.
Fly high on the thermals
And remember – double back your necks." *Mimi*, pg. 25

Fact: Great white pelicans can soar up to heights of 10,000 feet on thermal currents. Instead of stretching out their necks as geese and swans do, they lay their necks back on their shoulders.

White Pelicans

The pelicans are gone. Her friends have departed to their homes. Mimi sits on her branch long into the night, remembering...

"A new song was perched in her heart. She would keep it there until the pelicans returned. Until then, she 'would sing the song without the words and never stop at all'" *Mimi*, pg. 30

Mimi is a story of remembrance and hope and if ever birds need hope, it's on their migratory flights, where they fly thousands of miles without stopping and are vulnerable to attack, dehydration, towers, lighted skyscrapers, and wind tunnels.

Here is the rest of the poem which inspired the story of Mimi:

"And sweetest in the gale is heard
And sore must be the storm
That could abash the little bird
That kept so many warm.
I've heard it in the chillest land
And on the strangest sea,
Yet never in extremity
She asked a crumb of me." Dickinson

Book Six – *Ruddy: Living on the Wind*

After writing Mimi, I was smitten with migration. I read Scott Weidensaul's book, *Living on the Wind*, and began researching the amazing avian flying machines who chase summer twice a year:

The black-polled warbler is a 4-inch sprite and weighs .4 ounces (the equivalent of two quarters, 12 business cards, or an empty pop can). It flies over 10,000 miles a year, up to three days without stopping, 1700 miles in one "go," from the Arctic tundra to Patagonia and back. Skimming wooded peaks, skirting urban skyscrapers, and crossing vast stretches of open water in the Atlantic Ocean, where the fate of weak fliers is to fall into the waves and perish, the warblers can't glide, so they must flap. Their wings flap 20 times a second for a total of 3 million flaps in a trip at altitudes of 5000 ft. These avian wonders, whose feathers weigh more than their bones, are all heart and pure grit.

The red knot, banded B95, is dubbed the Moonbird because it travels the equivalent distance of to the moon and back.

The Arctic tern weighs three to four ounces and migrates 44,000 miles, back and forth from its home in the Arctic tundra, the longest distance of any animal in the world. Twice a year they fly a figure 8 hopscotch pattern from the Arctic, across the ocean to the coast of Africa, then back to South America, and on to Patagonia, following spiraling patterns in the atmosphere and avoiding flying into the wind. This plump little aerial meatball, in a 30-year lifespan, will travel the equivalent distance of three trips to the moon and back.

Guided by the sun, moon, and stars, polarized light, landmarks, a keen sense of smell, and little crystals in their birdbrains which orient them magnetically, over 5 billion birds – "guided missiles," take to the skies every spring and fall, weaving an incredible tapestry across the hemisphere. They fly mostly at night while braving challenges of satellite towers, skyscrapers, windmills, strobe lights, predators, dehydration, lack of food, and exhaustion.

Ruddy Turnstone

Book Six was germinating. The main character was a ruddy turnstone, I named Ruddy. For years I'd noticed ruddy turnstones at Pelican Cove, so named for "turning" or flipping stones to find food hidden underneath. The turnstones arrived in the spring, stayed about three weeks, and then disappeared. I hadn't given them much thought before, but now,

I began to wonder – where did the turnstones come from and where were they going when they suddenly disappeared from the cove?

Until now my research dealt with the aerial feats of migratory birds, but this year, watching the turnstones feverishly turning and flipping stones in search of food, made me realize the duality of migration – it's not just the aerial feats of the birds, it's also the importance of habitat and food supply to their flights that determines survival. Timing is everything.

When birds touch down after flying for days on end without food and water, they are seriously dehydrated and famished. They need nourishment quickly and efficiently. Following their navigation computer chips, they fly along main migratory routes because these are aligned with feeding grounds.

My story would feature not only the aerial feats of Ruddy, a turnstone, who's skip-hopping and feeding on his way home to the Arctic tundra from Patagonia and then flying across the Gulf of Mexico, where I spot him, at the cove, but also the importance of habitat and food supply to the success of his journey:

"…Ruddy lies dazed on the shell path, a heap of tortoiseshell feathers and bones, his heart barely beating. Exhausted from flying thousands of miles without stopping, without eating, without drinking, it feels like his wings are still flapping. 'Kek, kek, kek,' he croaks feebly. 'Hello, world. I'm here. I made it…'

After a time, Ruddy struggles to his feet, straightens, fluffs out his feathers, and totters over to the water for a drink. A song trills out of his throat as he anticipates filling his belly.

> 'Flip, flip, flip it high,
> Flip it right up to the sky.
> 'Kek, kek, kek,' what will I see?
> Waiting under this shell for me?'" *Ruddy: Living on the Wind*, pg. 2, 5

For nearly three weeks, I watch the turnstones gorge on the crabs, crayfish, and worms, they uncover beneath the shells and stones on the shell path.

"Then one night the cove comes alive with turnstones flapping and fluttering, squawking and squealing. A gust of wind gathers the birds into a whirling gyrating mass and with a giant whoosh thrusts them heavenward. Ruddy flings himself into their midst." *Ruddy: Living on the Wind*, pp. 9, 11

The cove is silent. Ruddy and his fellows are gone. I am left to write their story. By now I know where they have come from. I know they are headed to the Arctic mudflats, their summer home; however, since they need to stop for food on the way, I need to find out where they'll be stopping next. What I learn blows me away – on the wind!

And that part of the story, my friends, you'll have to find out by reading the book.

Ruddy Turnstones

Note: the Migratory Bird Act, passed in 1916, prohibited hunting during migration seasons. Until that time, migration was a heyday for hunters, as mass shootings led to the near extinction of many species, among them the passenger pigeon. Ruddy was published in 2016 and celebrates one hundred years of protected flight.

Book Seven – *Can We Nest Here?*
A Tale of Acceptance and Belonging

"'Dear world,
Can we nest here?
Raise our young, sing our song?
We don't just want to fit in,
The missus and I want to belong."
Regards, Mr. Limpkin'" Introduction, *Can We Nest Here?*

There it was – Book Seven, *Tales from Pelican Cove* series.

Once again I was a writer without a story; however, unlike Ruddy, I'd turned over stone after stone but had found no crabs or crayfish underneath.

The only thing giving me hope was knowing that Number Seven is the number of completeness and perfection, derived from God's creation.* I brushed aside any symbolic significance there might be in the fact that God rested on the seventh day.

It's said that guardian angels use signs to communicate with us and bring us important messages. If the Number Seven comes to you, it means that you must complete something you have started, but if I was to complete my series with a seventh book, wouldn't I at least have to have an idea?

The only idea I had, and it wasn't an idea as much as a sense, was that I had been ungracious and downright rude to a pair of birds in my books – the limpkins.

In *What Do You See, Mrs. Night Heron* and *Ossie the Brave Fish Hawk*, the limpkins are shunned by other birds for their constant raucous screams. Other birds don't want them around and they certainly don't want them nesting nearby, since the limpkins' "krowwing" could go on all night.

My description was justified. The limpkins' screams were used for jungle sound effects in the Tarzan films and the Hippogriff in the film *Harry Potter and the Prisoner of Azkaban*.

Still, it bothered me that I had dissed and disrespected them the way I had.

That spring I began reading the work of author/researcher Brene' Brown. Her work on vulnerability, acceptance, and belonging led me to think about the limpkins:

"True belonging is the spiritual practice of believing in and belonging to yourself so deeply that you can share your most authentic self with the world and find sacredness in both being a part of something and standing alone in the wilderness. True belonging does not require you to change who you are; it requires you to be who you are. It's not the belonging that comes with just joining a group. It's not fitting in, pretending, or selling out because it's safer. It requires us to be vulnerable, get uncomfortable, and learn how to be present with people without sacrificing who we are." Brown, Schawbel Interview, 2017

Wow. If anyone was vulnerable and needed acceptance and belonging, it was the limpkins. I'd make it up to them for my unflattering depictions and use them as heroes in my seventh book. Their story would help convey these important lessons to children.

Limpkin

My guardian angels were astir. I began my research.

In addition to their raucous cries, I learned that limpkins nest in the winter, the male builds the nest before pair-bonding with a mate, they feed almost exclusively on apple snails, and they build nests in a wide variety of places.

The story was underway. To portray as many shorebirds, in addition to the main characters, the limpkins, as possible, I included the white ibis, the oystercatcher, snail kites, red-eyed vireos, and the cowbird – birds that either lived and nested near the limpkins or had a similar diet. Counting Mr. and Mrs. Limpkin that added up to seven – the perfect number! The story bubbled and simmered along:

The story begins with the limpkins foraging for food on the shell path, partaking in their "pair-bonding" ritual; however, since, according to the research, the male builds the nest before mating, I would have to use a writing tool, known as "flashback." This allows Mr. Limpkin to recount, for his missus, the rejections he's suffered by the white ibis, the oystercatcher, and the snail kites (note the number of birds is three*). The reader is then brought back to the shell path.

The limpkins leave for home, but sadly, they have no home. Suddenly they hear a bird's song. It's the red-eyed vireo. Voila! The missus remembers something she's heard about vireos.

"In the branches of a live oak
The limpkins built their nest.
The vireos had no interest in apple snails
And they warbled all night – without rest!" *Can We Nest Here*, pg. 20

Limpkins

Their nesting problem is solved! Finally, a place where the limpkins belong!

To my delight, I learned that the cowbird, a pesky parasite and a minor character in the story, sneaks more eggs into red-eyed vireos' nests than the nests of any other bird. But not this year! The limpkins scared them away with their "krow-wing!" It was the perfect ending. Not only do the limpkins belong, but they're also valued!

"True belonging does not require you to *change* who you are; it requires you to *be* who you are." Brown

*Listing three entities, the white ibis, the oystercatcher, and the snail kites, helps the reader to remember information more easily. Combining brevity and rhythm with the smallest amount of information creates a pattern for the reader and allows the writer/speaker to appear knowledgeable while being both simple and catchy.

*About Number Seven.

There are 7 continents, 7 classical planets, 7 oceans, 7 vertebrae in the neck, 7 digits in a phone number (not counting the area code), 7 hills in Jerusalem, Rome, and Istanbul, 7 Liberal arts, 7 wonders of the ancient world, 7 layers of skin (2 outer and 5 inner), 7 colors in the rainbow (ROY G. BIV), 7 notes in the do-re-mi scale, 7 holes in your head, 7 directions, 7 candles in the Jewish menorah, 7 days in a week, 7 deadly sins, 7 virtues, 7 gifts of the Holy Spirit, and 7 is the number of games in a NHL, MLB, and NBA final.

In addition, ocean waves roll in 7's, a cube has 7 dimensions (including the inside), there are 7 days of creation, with God resting on the 7th day, 7 is mentioned 735 times in the Bible, with the majority occurring in the book of Revelation, the word "created" is used 7 times in the book of Genesis. Crashes in the stock market have occurred in 7-year cycles. The number 7 is important in Hinduism, Judaism, and Islam as well as in Christianity. That's just a start!

It is believed that our guardian angels use different signs to communicate with us and bring us important messages. If number 7 comes to you, it is a sign that you need to complete something you have started. You have the opportunity to use all your talents and natural abilities because the angels will help you reach your goals more easily.

An Anhinga Started the Journey

Have you ever heard of an anhinga? If not, you aren't alone. Author Janet Hasselbring had never heard of one either, until she watched it sitting on a perch in front of her Florida condo every day drying and preening its wings. Janet's experience with this water bird became the subject of her first book, *Andy Discovers Peanut Butter*, published in 2007.

Andy Discovers Peanut Butter was just the first in a series of seven children's books inspired by the incredible wild/shorebirds of Florida. The series, *Tales from Pelican Cove*, are based on Janet's experiences with different Florida birds. "I weave facts I gain from my research into the stories," she states.

Janet, her husband Don, and their Welsh terrier, Maggie May, are snowbirds who live in West Michigan during the summer months. Grand Haven's culture, history, parks, hiking and biking trails, are some of the reasons she loves the area. Maggie May is a therapy dog and they do "lots of therapy visits."

She grew up on a farm in New Era that is now Country Dairy, a fourth-generation farm with lots of history. In 2012, she wrote *Country Dairy, Looking Back Moving Forward* as a tribute to her parents. She wanted to make sure her three children and four grandchildren always remembered her parents for their faith, perseverance, and hard work.

She also wrote *In the Garden*, a memoir that portrays her mother's lifetime journey of faith and courage on the farm. This book was inspired by a class Janet took on writing memoir and personal story, and is the book nearest to her heart.

Her most recent book and the seventh in her *Tales from Pelican Cove* series is *Can We Nest Here?* This book, her favorite with regard to inspiration, is based on themes of acceptance, belonging, connection and vulnerability from the work of Author Brene' Brown. It is also based on the Dr. Seuss' quote – "Why just fit in when you were born to stand out?" Janet has been told that *Can We Nest Here?* is a "must read for parents and children."

Her successful ability to write for children may have come from her 36 years as an elementary grade teacher in the Grand Haven Area Public Schools district. She also taught music for almost 20 years, and directed SPARK, an arts education program, during part of her tenure.

If you are a regular reader of *Senior Perspectives Newspaper*, Janet's name may sound familiar. Writing short stories for SPN has become one of the major joys and mainstays of her life. She has earned numerous honors from the NAMPA Annual Awards Competition (which provides special recognition for excellence in senior publications) for her short stories and personal essays. She is currently in the process of having the stories published as a collection of short stories. In addition, Janet is working on a series of articles for SPN on How Does Your Garden Grow?

Tricia L. McDonald is an internationally published author, public speaker and writing coach. Her new middle-grade fiction book, <u>The Sally Squad: Pals to the Rescue</u> was published in March 2020. Her <u>Life With Sally</u> series: <u>Little White Dog Tails</u>, <u>Still Spinnin' Tails</u>, <u>Waggin' More Tails</u>, and <u>Princess Tails</u> are compilations of stories chronicling life with her miniature bull terrier. <u>Quit Whining Start Writing</u> is a guide to help writers put away the excuses and get the writing done.

Chapter 6
How Does Your Garden Grow?

"Gardens are not made by singing 'Oh, how beautiful,' and sitting in the shade." Rudyard Kipling

"What is a weed? A plant whose virtues have never been discovered." Ralph Waldo Emerson

"Weeds are flowers too, once you get to know them." A.A. Milne

"I want it said of me by those who knew me best, that I always plucked a thistle and planted a flower where I thought a flower would grow." Abraham Lincoln

"Remember that children, marriages, and flower gardens reflect the kind of care they get." H. Jackson Brown, Jr.

"The flower that smells the sweetest is shy and lowly." William Wordsworth

"The best place to find God is in a garden. You can dig for him there." George Bernard Shaw

How Does Your Garden Grow? I Hope is a Thing with Petals

"March is the month of proclamation," stated Emily Dickinson. Her garden comes to life after a long cold winter in Amherst, MA.

"Buds swell on the branches, elbowing into the longer, warmer days. Songbirds charm the trees. Dormant plants, metabolisms slowed during the long Massachusetts winter, wake up. The first flowers to bloom each year are the little bulbs." *Emily Dickinson's Gardening Life*, McDowell

What does March proclaim?

1. March proclaims Hope.

If hope is "a thing with feathers" – birds, to Dickinson, then it's also "things with petals" – bulbs. In autumn, we plant little food sacs, which rest dormant under the frozen ground, unseen for the remainder of the year, and then, Voila! they burst forth in spring in a profusion of color, stunning the landscape with beauty and hope, rewarding those who braved the cold autumn day with gloves and trowel.

Emily Dickinson a gardener? Her name brings to mind a well-known image of a sixteen-year-old girl in a white dress staring boldly out of a daguerreotype. Emily Dickinson the poet, of course; yet beyond the stuff of literary legend, Emily loved plants. The love of gardening inspired many of her poems. Her trowel and pen went hand in hand.

Crocuses

Her crocuses are "vassals" of the snow, and "martial" – standing in the frozen ground like soldiers.

Another of her favorites was the tulip, which she describes as asleep and forgotten, save by the gardener:

Tulips

"She slept beneath a tree –
Remembered but by me.
I touched her Cradle mute –
She recognized the foot –
Put on her Carmine suit
And see!" Dickinson 15 1858

And the daffodil. With usual cryptic clarity she pens :

"I dared not meet the Daffodils –
For fear their Yellow Gown
Would pierce me with a fashion
So foreign to my own –" *I Dreaded That First Robin So,* Dickinson

Daffodils

2. March proclaims Faith

I have a vested interest in bulbs. Last fall I knelt on the cold hard ground in my shade garden and gently placed pudgy little pouches into winter abodes with a prayer that in due time, they would awake from sleep, put on their colorful costumes, and "see!" I figured if St. Francis could preach to "things with feathers," I could invoke blessings on "things with petals."

Planting bulbs, in fact gardening in general, becomes a spiritual experience, when one realizes that just as flowers will emerge from the deadness of winter, so God raised Jesus from the dead on the first Easter, and will also resurrect those asleep in Him.

"Our Lord has written the promise of the resurrection not in books alone, but in every leaf in springtime." Martin Luther

The garden for me, like Emily, is my church. It's there I drink in the wonder of rebirth and ponder the cornerstone of my faith – the resurrection.

"Some keep the Sabbath going to Church –
I keep it staying at Home –
With a Bobolink for a Chorister –
And an Orchard for a Dome –
Some keep the Sabbath in Surplice –
I, just wear my Wings –
And instead of tolling the Bell, for Church –
Our little Sexton – sings.
"God" preaches, a noted Clergyman –
And the sermon is never long,
So instead of getting to Heaven, at last –
I'm going, all along." Dickinson 236, 1861

Bobolink

3. "and the greatest of these…"

March proclaims Love

A defining quality of Love is selflessness. Things with petals add beauty and color (and nectar!) to the world while asking nothing for themselves.

Plants above ground may not provide as dramatic a renewal as bulbs, but they too appear dead and lifeless during winter, only to sprout green with the coming of Spring.

"Just remember in the winter,
far beneath the bitter snows,
Lies the seed, that with the sun's love,
In the Spring becomes the rose." *The Rose*, McBroom

"A sepal, petal, and a thorn
Upon a common summer's morn.
A flash of dew, a bee or two –
A breeze, a caper in the trees –
And, I'm a rose!" Dickinson

Rose

How does your garden grow?

How Does Your Garden Grow? II As We Think, So We Are.

My garden is awash with color and alive with daffodils, crocuses, and tulips; just what I envisioned last fall when I braved the cold and placed hundreds of bulbs into the hard, partially-frozen ground.

Easter and the arrival of spring are especially poignant this year. I watch the miracle of new life in my garden and recall the words of Martin Luther, "God has written the promise of the resurrection not in books alone, but in every leaf in springtime."

Gardening involves grubbing in the dirt, pulling weeds, watering flowers, and planting bulbs and seeds. Gardening helps me realize a deeper truth – our thoughts are like bulbs that produce flowers; like seeds that produce crops.

In his book, *As a Man Thinketh,* based on *Proverbs 23:7,* James Allen claims our thoughts are the most important thing about us. All that we achieve or fail to achieve is the result of our thinking:

"Just like nothing can come from corn but corn and nothing from nettles but nettles, good thoughts and actions can never produce bad results; likewise bad thoughts and actions cannot produce good – a truth we understand in the physical world, but fail to grasp in the mental and moral world."

The analogy of gardening to matters of the heart has its roots deep (pun intended) in religious and secular literature.

In the parable of the sower, Jesus likens faith to the sowing of seeds. Seed falling on a barren path depicts faith without any substance; seed sown in rocky places is faith which falls away when trials and challenges arise; seed which falls among thorns describes faith which fades with competing worries and cares; but seed which falls on rich soil is like faith which hears the word, accepts it, and produces crops, up to a hundredfold.

Allen continues. "A person's mind may be likened to a garden, which is intelligently cultivated or allowed to run wild; but whether cultivated or neglected it will bring forth. If no useful seeds are put into it or if it is not tended, an abundance of useless seeds will fall therein and will continue to produce their kind."

The message is clear. If we strive to be holy we must control our thoughts and because emotions accompany thoughts, they become extremely powerful.

"Just like the underlying energy field forms atoms which then bind together into molecules and ultimately manifest into the physical universe, so all that goes on inside of us has its foundation in an underlying energy field. The movements in this field create our mental and emotional patterns as well as our inner drives, urges, and instinctual reactions. Call it Chi, Shakti, or Spirit, it's an underlying energy that flows in particular patterns through us." Michael Singer, *The Untethered Soul*

Because we cannot escape our thoughts, Singer cautions, "Once these energies capture your consciousness and all your powers of awareness focus on them, this power begins to feed them. Consciousness is a tremendous force. The thoughts and emotions on which you concentrate become charged with energy and power, becoming stronger the more attention you give them."

Jesus appropriately uses a tree to symbolize this power, noting that the barren fig tree symbolizes one who has little faith and like the tree, takes up space but bears no fruit. Contrast that image to the tree described by King David in Psalm 1:

"Blessed is he whose delight is in the law of the Lord…he is like a tree planted by rivers of water which yields its fruit in season and whose leaf does not wither."

In the memoir, *In the Garden*, I used that analogy to describe my father working his farm in the 1930s.

"As Henry walks back and forth across the field, behind the horses, he guides the planter as it drops seed corn into the furrows, reflecting on the Scriptures he's studied and memorized. Like the seeds that fall on rich tended soil, he becomes like an apple tree, planted by rivers of water, bearing its fruit in season…." *In the Garden*, pg. 25

How does your (mental) garden grow?

How Does Your Garden Grow? III
Bulbs, a Virus, and Quarantine

Emily Dickinson, planting seeds and bulbs in her garden, in Amherst, Massachusetts, muses, "How few suggestions germinate. Seeds are simpler than suggestions after all." How true.

Summer of 2020. I was planning to continue my garden series (begun that spring), for the July/August issue of Senior Perspectives, but how could I ignore the COVID-19 pandemic which was so drastically affecting our lives? A friend suggested I combine the two themes. Hmm, a "suggestion." Would it germinate?

While mulling it over I received a note from my friend. Knowing I love gardening, she interspersed puns into her message: "just one of rose things," "peas and quiet," "seed between the lines," "all dressed up and nowhere to grow," and "absolutely radishing."

Fueled by the puns, her suggestion (to combine the themes of gardening and the virus), began to germinate. Bulbs and seeds are storage organs, full of life and potential. They lie dormant in the winter, then bloom in the spring. That sounded a lot like us dealing with COVID-19.

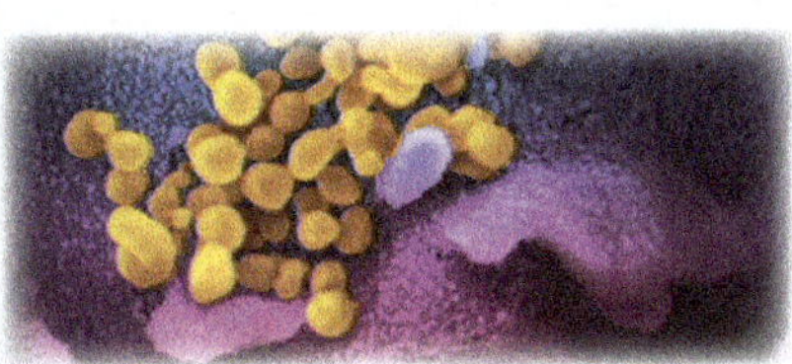

I asked friends to share stories of life in quarantine. It became apparent, from their stories, that we all were struggling to deal with our "new normal." I turned to two of my favorite authors for insight:

1. **Anne Morrow Lindbergh** wrote *Gift of the Sea* while vacationing on a Florida island. Alone and isolated, by choice, she was seeking solitude. Alone and isolated, with no choice because of COVID-19, we were struggling with loneliness and its handmaidens – despair, and depression.

"No man is an island," wrote Donne, describing the interconnectedness of all beings, but Lindbergh cautions that before meaningful connections with others can occur, we need to know ourselves. Being alone or isolated physically does not, in itself, imply loneliness. One can be isolated but feel close to others. Conversely, one can be with a friend and feel estranged, or hug a loved one and feel miles apart. Only when you are connected to your core, cautions Lindbergh, can you feel connected to others.

Bottom line? Being alone and *connected* (Lindbergh), promotes peace and spiritual harmony; being alone and *disconnected* (those of us in quarantine), spawns loneliness and can lead to despair and depression.

2. **Brene' Brown**, writer/researcher writes: "Wholeness is recognizing and celebrating that we are inextricably connected to each other by a power greater than all of us and that our connection to that power and to one another is grounded in love and belonging. Practicing spirituality brings a sense of perspective, meaning, and purpose to our lives ..." Interview, Dan Schwabel, 9/12/2017

My friends' stories

The prompt: How have you dealt with the quarantine? Did you learn something about yourself you didn't realize before? Is there one experience in particular that stands out?

Though the details differed, the stories had common themes: establishing daily routines with physical and mental exercise, maintaining health and hygiene, enjoying nature, undertaking a project, learning a new language or craft, keeping a journal, practicing faith and prayer, using Skype and Zoom with family members, especially grandchildren, reading aloud, and doing random acts of kindness. All agreed they'd learned to dig deep, finding strength and resources they didn't know they possessed. Many of them pledged to maintain their routine after the quarantine. Two stories stood out as especially poignant:

Gladys is 85. Her son-in-law stops by regularly to check on her. He's placed two chairs on the back porch, 6 feet apart and after finishing his jobs, he and Gladys sit and chat over a cup of joe.

Jean's husband, Peter, is failing physically and mentally. To keep his spirits up during the quarantine, Jean's initiated over a dozen "surprise driveway visits." One cool March afternoon, she sets up a visit with friends in Kalamazoo. As they head out, Peter tries to guess who they're visiting. Jean turns it into a guessing game with clues. Once they arrive, they remain in the car and chat with their friends, who sit outside, wrapped in blankets.

July 2020. My garden is ablaze with color. I'm especially pleased to see the lilies blooming. Free of the bulb encasements which bound them all winter, they stand straight and tall, braving the elements. One day, hopefully soon, we too will be free from the quarantine that's bound us this season and emerge stronger, more resilient, and more connected to ourselves and to others than ever before.

How Does Your Garden Grow? IV "The Genius of the Place"*

Genius and Gardening? Hmmm… I read two stories recently that got me thinking about how I might add a few touches of genius to my garden come spring.

1. The story, *Genius of the Place*, by Stephanie Barron (Jane Austin Mysteries),* is set in the summer of 1805, at Jane's brother Edward's palatial estate in Godmersham in Kent. A murder occurs at a horserace. The plot thickens as Humphry Repton (a murder suspect himself), is hired to improve the estate. His picturesque vision of transforming the English countryside introduces us to the world of landscape design/gardening, an underlying theme in the story.

In her series, Barron casts Austin as a sleuth. She incorporates real-life events gained from Austin's letters, blending fact and fiction into clever mysteries stemming from Austin's "wilderness" years, after her father died, leaving Austin, her mother, and sister shuffling from relative to relative.

"The landscape artist captured a distant prospect of an ancient hillside, surmounted by cypress and a few tumbled columns: the mood one of desolation and peace, a glorious past recalled and now thankfully put to rest." *The Genius of the Place*

Repton Pheasantry Design
at the Pavilions

Repton, last of the great 18th-century landscape artists, said, "All rational improvement of grounds is necessarily founded on dogged attention to the character and situation of the place to be improved." Alexander Pope agreed: "Consult the genius of the place in all."

In America, Repton's "genius" is evident in Central Park, Biltmore Estate, National Zoological Park, and the University of Chicago, to name a few of the many creations of his disciple, Fredrik Law Olmsted. Olmsted, calling himself a landscape architect, felt his projects differed significantly from those of "mere" gardeners in their "elegance of design" – the creation of a composition in which all parts were subordinated to a single, coherent effect. His garden classic is aptly named, *Genius of Place*.

Olmstead's Central Park

When touring the Isle of Wight, one of Repton's "picturesque visions," Olmsted exclaimed, "Gradually and silently the charm comes over us; we know not exactly where or how."

2. Hans Hugenberg knew about genius. A horticulturist and landscaper in Italy, he was the chief consultant for the government, advising on everything from the design of national parks to the layout of official residences.

"His gardens extended in balanced and regular patterns, but with a twist and flair distinctively his own. He blended sunlight and shadows, sunken ponds with sloping fields and tunneling arbors, straight lines with curving pathways, and curious steps. His only regret was that he had neither the time nor the space to have a garden of his own." *100 Bible Verses*, pg. 23

When he retired, Hans purchased a villa, outside of Rome, with a quaintly designed garden in the rear. Overgrown, crawling with rodents, and infested with weeds, the garden needed a master's touch.

Hans knew what to do. He traveled to Naples, where he found a sculpture of Christ at the moment of His ascension. Christ's hands are lifted upward in blessing, His feet on tiptoe as though leaving the earth, His eyes look lovingly downward at those left behind.

After bringing the statue home, Hans cleared the debris and laid a foundation, then set it in place and began designing his garden around the figure. Every plant, every path, every pond, was dictated by its character; every tree and flower selected in proportion and uniformity of the ascending figure of Christ; every line and lawn led the eye to the uplifted hands and downward gaze of Jesus. Weeds were pulled and rats evicted under the loving gaze of the risen Lord. All parts were subjected to a single coherent effect.

Jesus was the centerpiece of Han's garden; the genius of the place. May He reign in your mind, heart, and home this Christmas and every day.

As far as the genius of my place, stay tuned…

Hans Hugenberg's Garden

How Does Your Garden Grow? V
Lent and Easter "In the Garden"

1. My Garden

> "I come to the garden alone
> While the dew is still on the roses
> The voice I hear, falling on my ear,
> The Son of God discloses.
> And He walks with me and He talks with me
> He tells me I am His own.
> And the joys (*sorrows*) we share, as we tarry there
> None other has ever known." *In the Garden*, verse 1, C. Austin Miles,
> modification mine

In his hymn, Miles describes the first Easter morning in the garden where Jesus was buried, when Mary, mistaking Jesus for the gardener, walked and talked with her risen Lord.

The hymn is often dismissed as sentimental and unfit for vital corporate worship experiences; however, Miles intends us to see Mary's experience as one relived by anyone who confronts Jesus and realizes His presence in the daily "gardens" of their lives, reinforcing the truth that faith is a deeply personal experience.

In 2021, Easter will fall on Sunday, April 4; however, for many, the joy of Easter is directly proportionate to the solemnity of Lent. It is only when we realize the deep anguish of the cross – "My God, why hast Thou forsaken me?" that we can exclaim in joy and wonder: "He is not here; He has risen!"

2. The Garden of Gethsemane

Jesus, forsaken by His disciples, struggles to accept the Father's will that He suffer death and crucifixion. In His presence, I share my struggles, disappointments, and grief at those loved and lost, the most recent, the sudden death of my beloved Welshie, Maggie May, who left us much too soon.

"The Dying's have been too deep for me; before I raise my heart from one, another has come." *Letters*, Dickinson. The word, "deep," aptly invokes a vision of Dickinson drowning in a pile of loved ones. I know the feeling.

"One day in March 1912," Miles recalls, "I picked up my Bible; it opened to my favorite chapter, John 20 – the meeting of Jesus and Mary in the garden. As I read, I became part of the scene, a silent observer to that moment when Mary knelt before her Lord. Under the inspiration of this vision, I wrote the words of the poem, and that evening composed the music." *Forty Gospel Hymns*, Sanville

Throughout the hymn, Miles uses the senses to create an intimate atmosphere. The "dew" depicts both a glistening visual and implies dampness in the air. The auditory effects, he "speaks," and "sings" add to the distinct feeling that Mary's encounter could be ours.

Chapel of the Holy Cross, Sedona, AZ

3. The Garden Tomb

Easter morning. The stone is rolled away; the tomb empty.
"…the melody He gave to me, within my heart is ringing." Verse 2

"I'd stay in the garden with Him,
Though the night around me be falling,
But He bids me go through the voice of woe,
His voice to me is calling.
…the joys we share… Verse 3, *In the Garden*

In His presence, sorrows turn to joy and a melody rings in my heart. "How lucky I am to have loved so many, I miss so much." Winnie the Pooh

I could stay with Him in the Garden Tomb forever, but it's not to be. The spell is broken. He "bids me go," and take up the burdens of life, but with the Easter promise that "Because He lives, we too shall live." This life is not the end. Eternity awaits and one day all will be redeemed. I'll be reunited with those I've lost – even Maggie May.

"I come to the garden alone…" This year, keep Easter alive by "walking and talking" with Jesus, in the routines; in the "gardens" of daily life.

Note: Meeting with God is not a matter to be taken lightly. Aslan, a lion, is the God-figure in Lewis's *Narnia Chronicles*. When Lucy and Susan are to meet Aslan, Susan says, "Ooh…I'd thought he was a man. Is he – quite safe? I shall feel rather nervous about meeting a lion." "That you will dearie, and make no mistake," replied Mrs. Beaver. "If there's anyone who can appear before Aslan without their knees knocking, they're either braver than most or else just plain silly." *The Lion, the Witch, and the Wardrobe*

How Does Your Garden Grow? VI Down a Rabbit Hole with Winston Churchill

Freesia

I'm having tea in my garden with Winston. We're chatting about writing strategies that make his books and speeches famous. I'm a bit surprised he accepted the invitation, though I suspect he was eager to meet my new Welshie, Clementine. He's partial to the name because that's his pet name for Lady Churchill.*

Winston loves gardens. He was captivated by the tranquility of Chartwell, on Kent's western boundary. When he put down roots there in 1922, it became his spiritual home. Looking out over the Weald of Kent he remarked, "I bought Chartwell for this view." When Country and Duty called him away, as they frequently did, he fretted, "A day away from Chartwell is a day wasted."

Garden Wall at Chartwell

I refill his coffee mug and offer him another scone. It's a humble offering, for if he had his druthers, he would chase his hearty breakfast with a whiskey and soda, to moisten his throat, then head back to bed with a cigar to work until noon.

His food quirks are legendary. His convalescent diet calls for champagne, oysters, and mouthfuls of steak. Once he threatened to go to Chartwell alone. When Clementine reminded him it was closed and there would be no one to cook, he boasted, "Then I shall cook for myself. I can boil an egg. I've seen it done." (He didn't go.)

Winston perks up when I promise Country Dairy ice cream later. "Wonderful," he purrs, "Cream coats the sheaths of the nerves."

My garden is alive with color, bursting with Winston's favorite flowers and shrubs. He lights a cigar and we get to the task at hand:

1. <u>Use four alliterative adjectives.</u>

"…answer with a sullen, senseless, solid, stupid, 'NO,'" he smiles mischievously, recalling one of his speeches. "Now these freesias – fresh, fragrant, flirtatious, fantastic. And the anemones – alluring, attractive, azure, abundant." He perches on my wall, noting that he built garden walls at Chartwell.

Anemones

Dahlias

2. <u>Use one-syllable words.</u>

He looks lovingly at a row of dahlias. "Fair, fine, fresh, frail," he announces. "The hyacinths – blue, bold, bright, brash."

3. <u>Anaphora – use of the same words or phrases in successive sentences.</u>

Suddenly Winston stands, thrusts out his chest, and thunders: "Our aim? Victory! Victory at all costs; victory in spite of all terror; victory however long and hard the road may be…"

Tulips

I am spellbound, silent, lost in history. After a time, Winston stirs, casts off the spell, and sits down. "Imagine these tulips braving the forces of nature," he whispers. "We will stand in the storm; we will stand in the rain; we will stand in the wind; we will not be flattened."

4. <u>Use of obscure and archaic words.</u>

"When I see lords and ladies snoozing during my speeches, I use words like 'benignant' and 'snoozery' to wake them up." He takes a hefty chomp on the fast-dwindling cigar. "I'm awed by the fantasticalnesses of your garden," he smiles. "That'll get their attention."

5. <u>Chiasmus – a figure of speech, in which the grammar of one phrase is inverted in the next.</u>

"'In one way you're right, and in another, you're wrong' – one of my favorites," he chortles. He peers about. "Every garden has a snake, but not every snake is in a garden." I nod in approval, sneaking a surreptitious glance about the garden. I've never seen a snake here.

But he's beginning to tire. It's time for ice cream. He relinquishes his cigar for a bowl of Grandpa's Vanilla. All is quiet except for the occasional tweet of a bird and the click of the spoon on Winston's teeth as he luxuriates with his cream. Clemmie lays at his feet.

He licks the bowl clean, looking disconsolate. I'm tempted to offer seconds but Lady Churchill has made it clear that Winston is getting chubby. Accepting his fate, he grudgingly surrenders the bowl. "Ahhhh," he sighs, "Simply delightfuliscious!"

Churchill at Chartwell

*Churchill's two great loves were brown miniature poodles named Rufus and Rufus II (the II was silent). Once, when Rufus (I) accompanied Churchill to Buckingham Palace, he started padding into the Cabinet Room. "No Rufus," chided Churchill, "I haven't found it necessary to add you to the War Cabinet yet." At Chequers, Churchill covered the poodle's eyes when watching the scene in Oliver Twist, in which Bill Sykes attempts to drown his dog, Bullseye, saying, "Don't look now, dear. I'll tell you about it afterward." Rufus (II) reportedly had breath like a flamethrower, but he still ate with the family in the dining room, on a Persian rug, served by the butler. When his "darling Rufie," his "closest confidant," who heard everything, died in 1962, he was buried at Chartwell next to his beloved predecessor, Rufus (I). "The Ten Most Famous Dog and Owner Combinations in History," Country Life, Elwes

How Does Your Garden Grow? VII The Genius of My Place

In laying out a garden, the first thing to consider is "the genius of the place." Alexander Pope 1728

In my article, in this series, entitled "The Genius of the Place," I explore the concept of gardening and genius with examples of English landscape gardening and Hans Hugenberg's garden, which uses a statue of Christ to determine its overall design.

Churchill once mused, while looking out over his gardens, "I bought Chartwell for this view." I wonder – as I, or a visitor, view my garden, to what is the eye drawn? What is my garden's central theme? What is its genius?

I wish I'd had Pope's advice years ago when I started gardening, for I have not one but several options. I'll take inventory of my garden and perhaps one of them will emerge as its genius.

1. **The patio wall** is a backdrop; an aesthetic partition between the garden and the woods beyond; a ledge for displaying baskets of cascading Canterbury Bells and pots of blooming begonias.

2. **A pair of flamingoes** serve as a reminder of winters spent in Florida, as shorebirds. Totally out of their element anywhere north of south Florida, plastic lawn flamingos (*Phoenicopterus plasticus*) are an American cultural icon, introduced by artist Don Featherstone in 1957. In the 21st century, they've become endangered. Efforts are underway to revive the art form and I like to think we're contributing to that effort. In 2009, Madison, Wisconsin, named the plastic pink flamingo the city's official bird.

3. **The "guardian" cherub angel** perches atop a post, its prayerful pose a daily reminder of grace and gratitude for life.

4. **A stone bench** provides a sense of peace and serenity to the garden where one "can come apart and rest awhile."

5. **Creeping Charlie** – When I cleared the woods behind my garden, I uncovered four distinct raised areas or mounds, which I've planted with creeping Charlie. A rapid spreader,

Charlie is a green, matted plant, also known as ground ivy. It boasts a yellow flower in late spring. Charlie's leaves and flowers brighten up the woods and provide a lush luxuriant parklike backdrop for the garden.

Carolina Wren

6. **Bird feeders, birdbaths, and birdhouses** – the garden comes alive with birds dining at the feeders, splashing in the birdbaths, and flitting through the woods. Loved as symbols of freedom in flight and the free-throated ease of their singing (*Bright Wings*, Collins), they lift one's spirits and arouse the imagination.

7. **The wind chimes** – Blowing in the breeze, the subtle, soothing, sounds are calming; the melodious, bell-like tones generate a spiritual, meditative atmosphere.

8. **Stone path** – A rustic stepping-stone walkway adds interest and provides a way for me, and my guests, to walk through the garden without crushing the posies.

9. **Memorial stones** – Five large ornamental stones, two of which are memorials to dogs I've loved and lost, provide balance for the patio wall on the opposite side of the garden.

10. **Cairns** – These stacked piles of stones serve as memorials (along with the stones mentioned above) to those I've loved and lost.

I finish the inventory and take a fresh look at my garden. I must admit there is no one thing to which the eye is drawn, no central theme; yet, the hodgepodge of items I've built, planted, and assembled over the years has a pleasant quality, a satisfying appeal, a personal distinction. I claim this place; it is mine; it gives me joy.

"The glory of gardening – hands in the dirt, head in the sun, heart, one with nature. To nurture a garden is to feed not just the body, but the soul." Alfred Austin

That, my friends, is the "genius of my place."

How Does Your Garden Grow? VIII The Purest of Human Pleasures

Monet's Garden

"My garden is my most beautiful masterpiece." Monet

Monet was speaking of his garden at Giverny. In one hectare (two and one-half acres), he mixed simple flowers, such as daisies and poppies, with rare varieties, and crafted a garden full of perspectives, symmetries, and colors. Later he would add the pond with its famous Japanese bridge, covered with wisterias, other smaller bridges, weeping willows, bamboo, and the famous nympheas (water lilies), which would be the focus of his artistic creations for more than 20 years.

Water Lilies

By shaping his subjects before painting them, he created his works twice. Always looking for mist and transparencies, he dedicated himself less to flowers than to their reflections in the water; a kind of inverted world transfigured by the liquid element.

We're fortunate to have a miniature copy of Monet's garden in downtown Muskegon. (https://www.facebook.com/Monet-Garden-of-MuskegonMI-117791008268146/). Features of this lovely "pocket" garden include a pebbled walkway to a pond with a blue bridge and blue rose-covered archways. All flowers and shrubs in the garden are identical to those in Monet's garden. Other local memorial gardens include Heritage Memorial, Mike Miller Memorial, and the John J. Helstrom Memorial at Muskegon Museum of Art.

Memorial gardens such as Monet's, are planted for the specific purpose of remembering someone or something special. They often have a theme or focal point, but whatever the type of garden or its purpose, it exemplifies the idea that "The love of gardening is a seed that once planted never dies." Jekyll

Here are some of my favorites:

1. Meijer Gardens, Grand Rapids, Michigan, Olbrich Gardens, Madison Wisconsin, Chicago Botanic Gardens, Chicago, Illinois, and Selby Gardens, Sarasota Florida, are botanical gardens, dedicated to the collection, cultivation, preservation, and display of a wide range of plants labeled with their botanical names. Meijer Gardens is also known for its sculpture park and butterfly garden, Selby for its orchids, and Olbrich for its Thai Pavilion – the only one outside of Thailand, surrounded by gardens.

2. Many gardens focus on a single bloom. The Mable Ring-ling Rose Garden, a section of the Ringling estate, Sarasota, Florida, was founded in 1913. Italian is style, its circular de-sign is patterned after a wagon wheel. In Holland, Michigan, a palette of color heralds the arrival of spring and the Tulip Festival. Rows of tulips line the city streets and mass plant-ings fill beds in fields and local parks. At Windmill Island, the only authentic Dutch windmill operating in the U.S., over 100,000 blooms, and a mass planting of over 60,000 flowers, dazzle the eye.

Rose

Tulip Festival

3. The Emily Dickinson Garden in Am-hurst, MA, recreates flowers and plants loved and tended by the poet in her reclu-sive years.

4. While most gardens can instill a meditative, peaceful, spiritual, experi-ence, some have a special religious significance, such as the Garden Tomb in Jerusalem, where visitors view the empty tomb and the place where Mary met her risen Lord.

5. Some gardens have a special emphasis. One of my favorites is the lavender labyrinth and herb gar-den at Cherry Point Market in Mears, Michigan. It will take a couple of years before the lavender is back to its former splendor after it was destroyed by the 2019 polar vortex, but the herb garden at the center of the labyrinth is thriving and provides visitors a meditative, healing space.

Lavender

6. My favorite garden though is my little piece of paradise, where I can put-ter as I please. Whether you are working in your garden, or visiting one, the rewards are many – gardens keep you physically fit, relieve stress, make you happy, boost your health, create a healthy environment, produce oxygen, and are great for kids.

"God Almighty first planted a garden. And indeed, it is the purest of human pleasures." Francis Bacon, *Essays*. Indeed!

Early morning at Walden Pond

Chapter 7
Multifarious Stories

"Not that the story need be long, but it will take a long while to make it short." Henry David Thoreau

"Short fiction is the medium I love the most, because it requires that I bring everything I've learned about poetry – the concision, the ability to say something as vividly as possible – but also the ability to create a narrative that, though lacking a novel's length, satisfies the reader." Ron Rash

A "Maze" ing

Labyrinth: a single non-branching unicursal path which leads to a center then back out the same way.

Maze: a circuitous trail that may have one correct path but can also be multicursal. It's designed to trick travelers into hitting dead ends or losing their way.

Hampton Court Maze

Summer of 2019: I'm walking a labyrinth at Chautauqua, NY, working my way to the center when I remember… a memory so visceral, so vivid, it could have happened yesterday.

Summer of 1967: London, England. First stop on a European tour with my friend Judy, our travel bible, *Frommer's Guide to Europe on $5 and $10 a Day*, in hand.

We spend the first day acclimating ourselves to London. The next day we venture outside the city for a tour of Hampton Palace, on the Thames. As we're leaving the grounds, we notice a sign: "Hampton Court Maze," with what seems like a challenge in smaller font: "On average it takes 20 minutes to reach the center." It's mid-afternoon. We have plenty of time to walk the maze and catch the bus back to our hotel for the evening's entertainment. We're the last group to enter. This should give us pause, but we pay the admission and enter the maze.

We head down the path toward the center reading the brochure as we go. "Hampton Maze is the UK's oldest surviving hedge maze. Commissioned around 1700 by William III, it's a trapezoid covering a third of an acre. Originally planted using hornbeam, it was later replanted using yew. Before the creation of the Hampton Court Maze, unicursal or single path mazes were the most popular mazes in the UK; however, this one is a multicursal or puzzle maze, known for challenging and confusing visitors with its many twists, turns, and dead ends." Hmmm…

For Londoners, the Hampton Court maze is a rite of passage; a place their parents brought them to test their orientation skills. It seems we're facing a double challenge – getting to the center in 20 minutes and proving that we, Americans and adults have orientation skills equal to English children…

Soon we hear fragments of disturbing music, sardonic laughter, and whispered conversations echoing around us. Years later I'll recognize the music as *Jareth the Goblin King*, from the movie Labyrinth (a movie my husband and I would ban our children from seeing). Portrayed by David Bowie, Jareth is the powerful ruler of an otherworldly kingdom – a maze, which the protagonist Sarah (portrayed by Jennifer Connelly) must journey through to win back her brother Toby.

I read on: "Spooky sounds designed to heighten the experience of getting lost, will follow visitors onto the benches at the center, which have been made touch-sensitive."

If these statements are meant to instill confidence in visitors walking the maze, it's not working with us.

Forty-five minutes elapse and we haven't found the center. Another hour and the sun is setting behind the suffocating hedgerows of yew, creating eerie shadows. The tourists in our group are long gone.

Hampton Court Maze

A pleasant afternoon is unraveling fast. We're alone with the demonic laughter, the impending darkness, and encroaching hedgerows. Panic and claustrophobia set in. I want to claw my way through the hedges, but they're dense and tightly woven like mangrove bushes guarding the Florida coastline…

We step up the pace. Time to cheat and consult the brochure map. Too dark to read. Forget the center. We just want OUT!

New worries beset us. Does anyone know we're still in here? What if they close the maze leaving us here overnight? We meander wildly up and down paths. Desperate, we toss up a prayer. Can God even hear us in here?

Then, oh joy! A miracle! We see an opening ahead. Dead tired and emotionally drained, two and a half hours after entering, we stagger out into a spacious dusky London evening. The sign screams a farewell. "Beware: getting lost doesn't have to be scary – it can be entertaining." Wrong…

Back at the hotel, we check details for our evening entertainment. You've got to be kidding. We're going to be watching a travelogue of England's Best Mazes and Labyrinths.

A "Maze" ing.

Labyrinths: Peace on Earth, One Step at a Time

"The labyrinth awaits the sojourner –
almost calls {my} name –
Will you enter my simple boundaries
and journey my paths
One Step at a Time?"*

Labyrinth at Chautauqua, NY

It's Friday, July 1967. Chartres Cathedral, France

My friend, Judy, and I are in Paris, the second stop on our European trip. We flew over the English Channel from London on Wednesday and today we're touring the Cathedral. Approximately ninety kilometers southwest of Paris, Chartres Cathedral is a marvel of Gothic architecture, constructed over 26 years, beginning in 1145. It's now a UNESCO World Heritage Site.

Our tour ends in the nave where chairs have been removed revealing mammoth concentric circles set in the floor radiating out from a center. It's the famous Chartres labyrinth usually covered up and obscured by the chairs; however, lucky for us, on Fridays, it's uncovered and made available to tourists between 10 a.m and 1 p.m. from the end of Lent to All Saint's Day, November 1. I'm spellbound. Before today, I hadn't ever heard of a labyrinth and now here I am viewing one of the most splendid in the world!

Our guide invites us to walk the labyrinth but first, she gives us some historical background:

In Greek mythology, the Labyrinth was an elaborate confusing structure designed and built by the legendary artificer Daedalus for King Minos of Crete at Knossos. Its function was to hold captive the Minotaur, the monster eventually killed by the hero Theseus.

Today, however, labyrinths are unicursal, i.e. having only a single, non-branching path, which leads to the center, then back out the same way. They're ancient symbols that relate to wholeness, combining the imagery of the circle and the spiral into a meandering but purposeful path. Unlike mazes, which are puzzles (we'd learned about mazes the hard way at Hampton Court in London – see the accompanying article "A 'Maze' ing"), labyrinths have long been used as meditation and prayer tools, representing a journey to our personal centers and back again into the world.

One would expect a cathedral as impressive as Chartres to have a grand labyrinth and it does not disappoint – at 42 feet in diameter, it's the largest in the world. A cross, as the starting point in construction, gives the labyrinth its distinctive Christian meaning, which is why pilgrims have been making the journey to Chartres for thousands of years.

Visitors can walk a labyrinth in any way and for whatever purpose they choose, but today we're invited to join the pilgrims in our group, who are there on a spiritual quest.

Our guide explains the "Palms" approach:

1. Palms down – enter the labyrinth and walk to the center with palms down to center your thoughts and release any conflicts, issues, or concerns you are experiencing.

2. Palms up – walking out from the center with palms up to receive strength and guidance from God.

3. Palms together – as you leave the labyrinth and *reenter* the world, turn to face the center with palms together in a prayerful end to your walk.

We began to walk the sacred space – receiving, releasing, and reentering – a deeply spiritual experience I will never forget.

Since that day, I've walked labyrinths formal and informal, inside and outside, grand and simple; in churches, a friend's backyard, alongside a mountain path, on the edge of a beach, shrouded by trees deep in the woods, in a lavender garden, sometimes with the palms approach and other times simply a scenic walk, but always one step at a time:

One Step at a Time....
The labyrinth awaits the sojourner –
Almost calls {my} name
Will you enter my simple boundaries
And journey my paths
One step at a time?

Labyrinth at Chartres Cathedral

Straight ahead, yet winding and crooked
The curled road beckons to be trod –
reinforcing the uplifted
blessing the downtrodden
Maybe tears, maybe joy, maybe peace
One Step at a Time.

All who are heavy laden, come stand at the gate
All who are fragmented, place one foot down
and the other in front
All who find wonder in the commonplace,
Come travel the narrow rows
One Step at a Time.

Give up your burdens, your middle of the night worries
Lay a care on a silver craggy rock as you pass
and move on to the next,
the monotony will soothe you
One Step at a Time.

Moving inward,
The trail winds in and out
Muscles untensing,
The walker's job seems easy,
The cares tumble down
and hit the ground with imagined force
lightening the load on contact
One Step at a Time.

Step 48, step 49, many more to go
while curling toward center like
a snail into its shell
Motionless as last,
a wooden cross is sighted,
God's presence overwhelms
and envelopes the inner sanctum—
His peace now a cloister
on the journey half over
One Step at a Time.

The pause to discover
new perspectives to ponder
fresh eyes, lightened heart
the world is a wonder
with steps unencumbered
the pilgrimage rewinds
One Step at a Time.

The breathing is slower,
the feet touch down lower;
and easier on the road well-worn
The unknown, now familiar
the end is the beginning
the sad is now glory
All happening unexpectedly
One Step at a Time.

A twist inward
A transformation outward
A fresh view from fatigued eyes
All part of a simple design
of much complexity
with the whole greater
then the sum of its steps
All the while traveling
One Step at a Time.* *One Step at a Time*, Suzanne Moody

"One of my standard – and fairly true – responses to the question as to how story ideas come to me is that story ideas only come to me for short stories." Roger Zelazny

Albert Einstein was Autistic, Andy Warhol was a Hoarder, George Gershwin had ADHD

Hard to believe. The genius who discovered relativity and invented the formula, E=MC2, which foreshadowed the development of atomic power and the atomic bomb, was autistic. Einstein talked late and was a social misfit. He lacked empathy, had difficulty developing friendships, preferred to be alone, engaged in one-sided conversations, and was preoccupied with his own interests. A difficult student, he's Calvin (Calvin and Hobbes), who raises his hand in class, and yells "BORING." On the way to the principal's office, he mutters, "Kill the messenger…."

Another shocker. A striking photograph of Warhol's dining room, taken shortly after he died, shows complete chaos. For more than 30 years, from about 1974 until the end of his life, Warhol filled cardboard boxes called "Time Capsules," with random items like receipts, letters, notes, photos, and Campbell soup cans – the inspirations and paper trail of his best-known works. The containers reveal Warhol's compulsion to save food scraps, dead insects, and invitations to events he didn't even attend.

George Gershwin

George Gershwin? He must have driven his parents and teachers nuts. A continual bundle of energy, he's the boy fidgeting with his pencil, unable to sit still and concentrate.

In a scrupulously well-researched look at the evolution of mental health, journalist Claudia Kalb gives readers a glimpse into the lives of twelve high-profile historic figures. Citing Einstein's autism, Gershwin's ADHD, and Warhol's hoarding, among others, Kalb provides compelling insight into a broad range of maladies. Her narrative brings a new perspective to one of the most compelling issues in today's cultural conversation: how much "disorder" is tolerable in an individual, how much will our culture allow, and what is the balance between disorder, psychoanalysis, and medication?

I'm feeling uncomfortable. I recognize myself, and people I know, in the lives of these individuals. I have stacks of clothes I haven't worn in a year, I talk to myself, and I like my "alone" time. I fidget when I'm bored, but that's the point of the book: where is the fine line between mental disorder and odd behavioral quirks?

Warhol's Campbell Soup Cans

Though Warhol embraced his disorder as part of his creativity, a key feature distinguishing hoarding from run-of-the-mill cluttering (which leads to its dysfunction), is that living spaces become so deluged with possessions they cannot be used for their intended purpose. Whew, I guess I'm okay on that one…

Gershwin would be the one, out of every ten children, between the ages of 4 and 17, diagnosed with ADHD, and among the 3 ½ million people taking meds. The meds don't always work and they can have harmful side effects, prompting critics to question pharmaceutical companies' motives.

Dr. Hallowell has dealt with ADHD patients for over 30 years. He disagrees that they are incapable of focusing. "What they need," he notes, "is a passion big enough to rein them in." When Gershwin found the piano, he became hyper-focused. On medication, we may never have heard the rhythms, color, humor, exuberance, and *hyperactivity* of *An American in Paris*, or the richly American piece, *Rhapsody in Blue*.

Abraham Lincoln was extremely melancholy, according to Kalb. Many historians claim the course of history may have been altered if Lincoln had been on Prozac for his melancholia. His unique gifts of sensitivity, empathy, and insight, while they contributed to his depression, were also indicative of his greatness, and may have been the very qualities that enabled him to guide our country through the Civil War.

One historian quips that Poe, on Prozac, when spying the Raven, might have bantered, "Hello birdie!"

Hallowell admits the difficulty in diagnosing a true behavior disorder and cautions parents, teachers, and psychologists, to consider a meticulous history from parents and teachers and to be judicious with prescribing drugs before trying alternative remedies.

Einstein's brain lies in the Mutter Museum, in Philadelphia. Visitors can view the thin slices of tissue once residing in the head of one of the greatest geniuses of all time. Dr. Rorke-Adams, a neuropathologist, donated the remains after studying them for over 30 years. What impressed her was their pristine quality. "The neurons were absolutely exquisite," she noted. "It looked like the brain of a child."

Youth distinguished Einstein's brain from the average. Untamed by the advance of years and aging, it was the essence of how Einstein lived and how he thought. In his words: "The pursuit of truth and beauty is a sphere of activity in which we are permitted to remain children all our lives."

Einstein on medication for autism? The thought should give us pause...

The book *Andy Warhol Was a Hoarder*, Claudia Kalb.

Teacher alert! Albert Einstein was Autistic

Summer is over. In a few weeks, area children will head back to school. Teachers beware! Among the children on the playground, walking the hallways, and in your classrooms, there may be a Charles Darwin, a George Gershwin, a George Jorgensen, an Abraham Lincoln, or just maybe, an Albert Einstein. Well… okay, a child or student who has anxiety, hyperactivity, hoarding issues, melancholia, or autism/Asperger's syndrome – traits often characterized as mental disorders today, but in these historical greats, traits which helped them make unique contributions to society.

In her book, *Andy Warhol was a Hoarder,* Claudia Kalb describes the disparity between the inner and outer lives of twelve historical figures and the inseparable connection of the two, seeking to give readers a better understanding and appreciation of the entanglement of genes, life experiences, and environmental risk factors that contribute to mental health disorders and the medical research aimed to alleviate the stigma and suffering they can cause.

The implications of her work for education are obvious. We recognize ourselves, and children and adults we know, in the traits of these individuals, but, more importantly, these individuals attended school – they played on playgrounds, walked hallways, sat in classrooms. We could have been their teachers!

As a former teacher, I wonder how I would have dealt with Einstein, a difficult student by all accounts! He talked late, was a social misfit, exhibited a lack of empathy, had difficulty forming friendships, preferred to be alone, engaged in one-sided conversations, and was preoccupied with his special interests – all red flags for psychoanalysis and possibly medication.

Einstein, along with Henry Cavendish, who discovered hydrogen, Newton, Marie Curie and her daughter, theoretical physicist, Paul Dirac, and countless others, suffered from one of the fastest-growing mental disorders of today – autism and Asperger's syndrome. Einstein was bored with school and did not attempt to mask it, making his teachers defensive and impatient with him. He is Calvin (Calvin and Hobbes), raising his hand, yelling "Boring!" Moments later, as he's marched off to the principal's office, he mutters to the world at large, "Yeah, yeah, kill the messenger…." I cringe. Could that have been my classroom?

Gershwin would probably have driven me crazy. I'm sure his parents were relieved to ship him off to school. A continual bundle of energy, he is the little boy fidgeting with his pencil, not able to sit still and pay attention. Today, he would be the one child out of every ten between the ages of 4 and 17 diagnosed with attention deficit hyperactivity disorder (ADHD). The ratio of boys to girls diagnosed with this malady is 3 to 1. Why is that, we, educators should ask. Have we pathologized normal childhood activity?

More than three and a half million people take meds for ADHD. The meds don't always work and have harmful side effects, prompting critics to question profit-hungry pharmaceutical companies' motives.

Dr. Edward Hallowell, a psychiatrist, has been dealing with ADHD children and adults for over 30 years. He suffers from the disorder himself. He considers the intense energy of ADHD a positive trait, using analogies to explain what's going on in the minds of his patients. "You have a Ferrari for a brain and bicycle brakes," he tells one. He compares the tremendous power and energy of ADHD to Niagara Falls. "The water force is phenomenal. It just needs to be harnessed to make it productive."

He disagrees with the claim that ADHD patients are incapable of focusing. "What they need is a passion big enough to rein them in. When bored, the ADHD mind will wander like a toddler on a picnic…it goes wherever curiosity leads it without regard for danger or authority," but when these individuals are captivated by what they love, they become hyperfocused and can concentrate better than even the quietest of contemplatives.

Good thing Gershwin became intrigued and obsessed with music and the piano or we'd never have heard the rhythms, color, playfulness, exuberance, and (hyper) activity of *An American in Paris*, or the richly American *Rhapsody in Blue*. Did I mention Gershwin was a school dropout?

I reflect on the students I've had in class, over my thirty-five years of teaching, and wonder how many geniuses I've tried to stifle. Perhaps I shouldn't be so hard on myself. Teaching is challenging! We take what parents send us. We have a classroom of children to teach. We need to maintain a degree of order. We have test scores to deal with and our tenure depends on the results.

While teachers chafe at the rigid structure and guidelines, the homogenized set curriculum driving a style of teaching that caters to the average student, allowing little individuation for children on either end of the learning spectrum, these are the reality in many school districts. Hopefully, I would have targeted at least one of these students – Einstein, Gershwin, or Warhol, as gifted and talented; however, these programs are becoming rare and far too often, the very areas which would give these challenging students that "passion big enough to rein in their activity," – visual art, music, dance, photography, specialty classes, etc., are reduced by budget cuts.

Lastly, there's the comfort level and personality of the teacher. How comfortable am I with a student who is difficult to teach? Do I appreciate and attempt to understand the child who doesn't fit the mold? In the end, this is the only factor we, teachers, can control, but it is the most important one since we stand at the front lines of a child's education.

Hallowell acknowledges the difficulty in teasing out a "true" behavior disorder. He's not suggesting that ADHD and autism don't exist; however, we need to be careful when deciding whether or not to refer a child to the school psychologist and the psychologist needs to be cautious in making a diagnosis requiring psychotherapy and/or medication. A diagnosis of ADHD or autism, Hallowell suggests, requires a detailed history from parents and teachers. It requires being judicious about prescribing drugs before trying alternate therapies. We might be medicating an Albert or a George.

Or an Abraham. Some historians speculate that Lincoln's unique qualities of sensitivity, empathy, and insight, indicative of his greatness, ran hand in hand with the pain of his melancholia; however, these were the very qualities that enabled him to guide our country through the Civil War. How might the course of history have changed if Lincoln had been on Prozac? One historian quips that Poe, on Prozac, might have seen the Raven and chirped, "Hello birdie!"

Einstein's brain – thin slices of tissue that resided in the head of one of the greatest geniuses of all time – lies in the Mutter Museum in Philadelphia. Dr. Lucy Rorke-Adams, a neuropathologist at Children's Hospital in Philly, donated his remains after studying them for over 30 years. What impressed her about Einstein's brain was its pristine quality. "The neurons were absolutely exquisite," she noted, "it basically looked like the brain of a young person."

Youth may be what distinguishes Einstein's brain from the average. Untamed by the advance of years and aging, it is the essence of how Einstein lived and how he thought – his soaring intellect powered by a childlike curiosity and wonder. In his words: "The pursuit of truth and beauty is a sphere of activity in which we are permitted to remain as children all our lives."

Isn't this what education should be about? Pursuing truth and beauty. Keeping those brain neurons childlike. Could there be more fitting mandates for teachers as a new school year begins and we welcome America's future into our classrooms?

The book: *Andy Warhol was a Hoarder*, by Claudia Kalb

"Short stories can be rather stark and bare unless you put in the right details. Details make stories human, and the more human a story can be, the better." V. S. Pritchett

If I Had a Bucket List...

I don't have a bucket list, though if I had one, I could cross off three adventures I enjoyed in the Yucatan this winter with my son and family. One day, my grandsons chose to go zip lining, snorkeling, and swimming with the dolphins, things I had never done, but I was there to spend time with them, so instead of exploring the famed archaeological site at Chichen Itza, with other senior tourists, I tagged along with my grandsons.

1. Zip Lining

We disembark from our tour bus, change into swim gear, strap into harnesses, and are promptly herded into line. This all happens so quickly, I don't have time to think about what I'm in for – I meekly follow directions and try to act like this is no big deal. Hey, I do this every day.

Like bighorn sheep, we trek upwards to a dock, sixty feet above a cove bordered by mangroves. After traversing a high-ropes circuit of hanging bridges, we arrive at the first zip line. I watch, fascinated, as one by one my family members are hooked onto the line and pushed off. Then it's my turn. That's when I think of my bucket list. I make a mental note to include zip lining on the list when I return home – if I get home!

My family is waiting for me on the other end. It's too late to back out now. I feel a rush of adrenaline as the guide gives me a shove. I take off, soaring

across the cove towards the opposite dock, where I come to an amazingly gentle landing. Three more jungle gyms and zip lines and this part of our adventure is over. Darn! I'm just getting the hang of it!

If only I had a bucket list...

2. Snorkeling

Next we climb aboard a watercraft. We're headed for a shipwreck. I spot the snorkeling gear underneath the benches upfront. How hard can snorkeling be? The boat and its captain seem seaworthy enough, which is comforting because once we leave the inlet, we're charging full throttle into the choppy turquoise waters of the Caribbean. We hunker down for a rough ride. Anchoring upstream from the shipwreck, our guide throws us our snorkeling gear and advises us to be aware of the strong current.

I'm still puzzling over my equipment, when my family members jump overboard. Hastily, I don my mask, clamber to the edge of the boat and leap in. Immediately I'm engulfed by giant waves. I swallow buckets of salt water. Gamely, I attempt a supine position, but the current is so strong, I'm tossed about like a balloon at a commencement ceremony. I've totally lost track of my family. The shipwreck is nowhere in sight. I'm contemplating asking for a refund, when another wave sends me under. Forget snorkeling. This is about survival.

Coughing and sputtering, I'm carried swiftly downstream, where I crash into jagged rocks surrounding the shipwreck. "Stay off the rocks!" someone shouts. *Not on your life!* The rocks are scraping and gouging my legs, but I feel safe here. Suddenly our guide appears with a life ring. "You stay with me!" he says. *You got that right!* I grab the ring with a death grip and he eases me away from the rocks. I have the presence of mind to ask if my family members are okay and accounted for. My grandsons glide by calling, "This is great! You okay Grandma Jan?" On the way back, the guide gives me an on-the-spot lesson: "If water enters the snorkel, simply exhale and you'll force the water out through the valve." *Of course. I knew that! Now he tells me!*

Exhausted, we tumble into the boat and shed our gear. I want to heave mine into the sea. Our guide counts heads to make sure all five of us are accounted for. My grandsons, agog with excitement, share the wonders of snorkeling through the shipwreck. My son has withstood the current and is eager to give it another try. "I almost drowned," my daughter-in-law says quietly. I have nothing to say.

We settle in and head for a reef. I make sure the nose pocket of my mask is snug and the mouthpiece fits comfortably between my teeth and ease overboard. The water is calm here but the guide isn't taking any chances. We're connected at the hip. The shipwreck becomes a distant memory, as I explore the magic of an underwater world inhabited by multicolored fish, brain coral, reef sharks, sting rays, and sea turtles.

If I only had a bucket list…

3. Swimming with dolphins on Isla Majereres

Finally, something safe and peaceful unless Greta, our friendly dolphin and her trainer have tricks up their sleeves! I've watched and admired dolphins in the Caribbean and Gulf of Mexico for years. Now I'm swimming and frolicking with one! We hug Greta and kiss her moist nose. It's breathtaking. We hear her 'blow' at the surface of the water as she exhales and then inhales fresh air. Each of us gets a ride on Greta's back. We dog paddle to stay afloat as she cuts and slices through the water, expertly hoisting us onto her slick smooth back and then dipping and whirling back to the trainer. I'm proud I didn't disgrace my grandsons by slipping off! Once playtime is over. Greta bids us farewell with a fountain of spray, forcefully breathing out and clearing away any water resting on top of her blowhole.

If I only had a bucket list…

"We get so many people saying short fiction is not economical, that it doesn't sell; but there are so many of us enjoying writing it and reading it. So it's wonderful to be around people who love short fiction too – it's like hanging around with my tribe." Junot Diaz

I Think I Can, I Think I Can

Fact 1: States plan the number of jail cells they will need based on the number of children not reading at the end of third grade.

Fact 2: Getting books in the home and encouraging parents to spend time with their children with books and literacy is a greater indicator of academic achievement and success in life, than intelligence.

Dolly Parton's Imagination Library (DPIL), is an international early childhood literacy program, which provides the gift of a book, FREE, every month, through local affiliates, to all registered children, from birth to age 5. The books are mailed to their homes, in their names.

A child, starting at birth, can receive sixty books by the time they start kindergarten, the first book, *The Little Engine that Could*, and the last book, *Watch Out, Kindergarten, Here I Come!* The books are chosen by a blue-ribbon panel of educators and are geared to the developmental level of the child. The cost of the books and mailing, approximately $2.00 per month or $25.00 annually, is covered by local community affiliates, who recognize 1. that the gift of a book to a child and his/her family is a gift to the community and 2. a community is only as strong as its weakest members,

Compare that with the cost of incarceration for a year and you'll have to admit, $25.00, spent on early childhood literacy, is a bargain.

Dr. Ben Carson, neurosurgeon and cabinet head of Housing and Urban Development, attests to the power of having books in the home. Ben and his brother, an astrophysicist, were living on the streets, with drugs, crime, and eventually prison, in their future. Their mother, wanting her sons to have a better life than she had, required them to read two books a week and write written reports for her, even though she could barely read them. "Between the covers of a book, I could go anyplace, be anybody, and do anything," recalls Dr. Carson. Books changed his life.

Dolly Parton grew up in poverty in rural Tennessee. She saw how her family, friends, and relatives in Sevier County struggled to read and how illiteracy negatively impacted their lives. Whatever the reasons that parents feel apathetic, disenfranchised, disinherited, and marginalized, Dolly was determined to remove at least one of the obstacles prohibiting them from rising above their circumstances and giving their children a "leg up" in life: books and literacy.

She credits her father as the inspiration for the DPIL. Illiterate himself, he encouraged Dolly to find a way to motivate families to read to their youngsters and ensure that no child/family would be without books. Today the Imagination Library is international, mailing over 50,000,000 books a year to preschoolers all over the world.

Local affiliates of DPIL pay for the cost of the books, register eligible children in their designated area, and manage the local database. Learn how your community can become an affiliate of the Imagination Library at dollypartonimaginationlibarary.org

Note: Since I wrote this article, Dolly Parton's Imagination Library has traveled to rural Oceana County in west Michigan, home of Country Dairy, where I grew up. Like Sevier County, in Tennessee, where Dolly Parton lived and began the program, poverty, poor school attendance, and high rates of illiteracy prevail. With Country Dairy as the proud champion of the Imagination Library, one thousand of the fourteen hundred seventy eligible children have been enrolled in the program. The Dolly Parton Imagination Library is alive and well in Oceana County!

"I'll give you the whole secret to short story writing. Here it is. Rule 1: Write stories that please yourself. There is no Rule 2." O. Henry

Jack be Nimble, Jack be Quick…

What's in a name? A lot, it seems, especially if your name is Jack. I've been intrigued by the name ever since my first grandson was named Jack seventeen years ago. Derived from *Jackin* (earlier *Jankin*), a medieval diminutive of John, it was common and became a slang word meaning "man." It's now regarded as an independent name, as it is for my grandson.

Jack is the subject of many a nursery rhyme, e.g. Jack be Nimble, Little Jack Horner, Jack and Jill, and Jack Sprat, and the beloved fairy tale, Jack and the Beanstalk. It's a name for fictional characters such as Jack Skellington, a Halloween movie character, Jackstaff, a British superhero, Mr. Jack, a comic strip (1903-1935), Jack Pumpkinhead, a character from the land of Oz, and the notorious legendary killer, Jack the Ripper.

Famous Jack namesakes include President John F. Kennedy (a.k.a. Jack), Emmy Award winner, Jack Benny, Oscar Award winners Jack Nicholson and actor/comedian Jack Lemmon, musician, Eddie Fisher (a.k.a. Jack), golfer Jack Nicklaus, boxer Jack Dempsey, up and coming tennis player, Jack Sock, author, Jack London, and more. Jack Ruby stepped out of a crowd and shot Lee Harvey Oswald, the accused assassin of John F. Kennedy, as Oswald was being transferred from a city jail to a country jail in Dallas. (Incidentally, the gray fedora Ruby was wearing when he shot Oswald sold for $53,775 at a Dallas auction. The shackles Ruby wore when dying at Dallas' Parkland Memorial Hospital sold for over $11,000, while an X-ray of Ruby's head went for more than $700!)

We turn pumpkins into Jack o lanterns, do Jumping jacks to stay healthy, surprise a grandchild with a Jack in the Box, look for a surprise in a box of Cracker Jacks, use car jacks to fix flat tires, pick jack-in-the-pulpits in the woods, walk Jack Russell terriers, try to beat the dealer in Blackjack, eat Apple Jacks for breakfast, admire the Jack Pines in Northern Michigan, plug our devices into phone jacks, fish the Great Lakes for jack salmon, and chew Black Jack gum.

So if someone asks, "What's your claim to fame?"

A lot it seems, if Jack is your name!

Amberjack is a Florida fish

A flapjack is a pancake on a dish.

You embellish your taco with Monterey Jack cheese.

A hijacked car is one you've seized.

A jackal is a long-legged wild dog.

A jack bean is a legume growing in a bog.

Applejack is fermented cider, a shade of pale yellow.

A Jack-a-Dandy is a little foppish fellow.

A Black Jack oak is a kind of tree.

Jack Hills – a range in Argentina I see.

Jackfruit is a tropical fruit, like a pear.

Jackboot is military footwear.

Jackdaws are small black crows.

Jack-by-the-Hedge plants grow in hedgerows.

A jack is a face card in a deck you deal.

A car jack is a device to lift a car you steal.

A jack-in-the-pulpit is a flower in the woods.

A cheapjack is a peddler of cheap goods.

A jackalope is a mythical antlered rabbit

Blackjack is a game that can easily become a habit.

A jackass is a pack animal, nimble and fast.

A Crossjack is a squaresail, a ship's mizzenmast.

A Jackapoo is a Jack Russell Terrier/Poodle mix

A jack is a male donkey who's just turned six.

A blue denim jacket is a piece of apparel.

Jack Daniels is a whiskey brand sold in a barrel.

Brrrrrr. Jack Frost is cold personified.

A Crackerjack is an expert at something, a guide.

I've written this quickly; the tale is now done –

Written before you can say "Jack Robinson!"

"Maybe stories are just data with a soul." Brene' Brown

The Limpkins* and the Wisdom of Brene' Brown**

"You are imperfect, you are wired for struggle, but you are worthy of love and belonging." Brown

"'Dear world,
Can we nest here?
Raise our young, sing our song?
We don't just want to fit in,
The missus and I want to belong.
Regards, Mr. Limpkin'" Introduction, *Can We Nest Here?*

There it was – Book 7, *Tales from Pelican Cove*, a series of books portraying wild/shorebirds of Florida and beyond. When I wrote Book Six, *Ruddy: Living on the Wind*, I thought I was finished with the series since I hadn't had any new ideas in a while. If the writing gods saw fit to send me one, I'd consider it – otherwise, I was done.

While I was on the prowl for a book idea, a friend suggested I read the work of author/researcher Brene' Brown. Her work on vulnerability, acceptance, and belonging, led me to think about the limpkin birds. If anyone was vulnerable, it was the limpkins. Perhaps the writing gods were stirring...

"Vulnerability is not about winning or losing. It's having the courage to show up even when you can't control the outcome." Brown

I'd included the limpkins in two of my previous books, *What do You See, Mrs. Night Heron* and *Ossie the Brave Fish Hawk*, albeit somewhat ungraciously. Other birds shunned them because of their loud raucous screams, which could go on all night long; they certainly didn't want the limpkins nesting nearby.

My unfavorable descriptions were justified. The Limpkins' "krowws" were used for jungle sound effects in the Tarzan films and for the Hippogriff in the film, *Harry Potter and the Prisoner of Azkaban*. Still, Brown's themes of compassion, connection, and courage suggested that I shouldn't have dissed and disparaged them as I did.

"You cannot shame or belittle people into changing their behaviors." Brown

Brown's work gave me an idea. If anyone needed acceptance and belonging, it was the limpkins. I'd make it up to them for my unflattering depictions and use them as heroes in a seventh book. Their story would help convey these important lessons to children, parents, and teachers. I'd have them "show up and be real."

"Authenticity is a collection of choices that we have to make every day. It's about the choice to show up and be real. The choice to be honest. The choice to let our true selves be seen." Brown

My research revealed that along with their raucous cries, limpkins nest in the winter, the male builds the nest before pair-bonding with a mate, they feed almost exclusively on apple snails, and they build nests in a wide variety of places.

The writing gods were awake now. The story was bubbling and gurgling along. To portray as many shorebirds, in addition to the main characters, the limpkins, as possible, I included the white ibis, the oystercatcher, snail kites, red-eyed vireos, and the cowbird. These were birds that either lived and nested near the limpkins or had a similar diet.

The story begins with the limpkins foraging for food and participating in their pair-bonding ritual, making them well, a pair.

"We don't have to go it alone. We were never meant to." Brown

Mr. Limpkin then recounts for the missus, his attempts to build a nest and his rejections by the white ibis, the oystercatcher, and the snail kites.

"The willingness to show up changes us it makes us a little braver each time. Courage is a habit, a virtue: you get it by doing courageous acts even when you don't feel courageous. Just like you learn to swim by swimming, you learn courage by couraging." Brown

After the flashback, the reader is brought back, once again, to the shell path. The limpkins leave for home, but sadly, they have no home. Suddenly they hear a bird's song. It's the red-eyed vireo. Voila! The missus remembers something she's heard about the vireos. Their nesting problem is solved:

"In the branches of a live oak
The limpkins built their nest.
The vireos had no interest in {apple} snails
And they warbled all night – without rest!"
Can We Nest Here, pg. 14

Imagine my delight to learn that the cowbird, a pesky parasite, and a minor character in the story, sneaks more eggs into red-eyed vireos' nests than nests of any other bird. But not this year! The limpkins scared them away with their "krowwing!" It was the perfect ending. Not only do the limpkins belong, but they're also valued!

"True belonging is the spiritual practice of believing in and belonging to yourself so deeply that you can share your most authentic self with the world and find sacredness in both being a part of something and standing alone in the wilderness. True belonging does not require you to change who you are; it requires you to be who you are. It's not the belonging that comes with just joining a group. It's not fitting in, pretending, or selling out because it's safer. It requires us to be vulnerable, get uncomfortable, and learn how to be present with people without sacrificing who we are." Brown, Schawbel Interview, 2017

*As portrayed in *Can We Nest Here?* Book Seven, *Tales from Pelican Cove*

** Brene' Brown, a research professor at the University of Houston, is best known for her famous TED talk, "The Power of Vulnerability." Brown has spent nearly two decades studying courage, vulnerability, shame, and empathy. All of her groundbreaking findings were included in five books that have become #1 *New York Times* bestsellers: *The Gifts of Imperfection, Daring Greatly, Rising Strong, Braving the Wilderness,* and *Dare to Lead.* "The Power of Vulnerability" is about expanding perception and embracing our imperfections. Brown's approach on how to cultivate courage, compassion, and connection turned a data presentation into one of the top five most-viewed TED talks of all time. Brown has become an inspiration for millions of people around the world.

"In short stories there's more permission to be elliptical. You can have image-logic, or it's almost like a poem in that you can come to a lot of meanings within a short space." Karen Russell

Listening Aids?

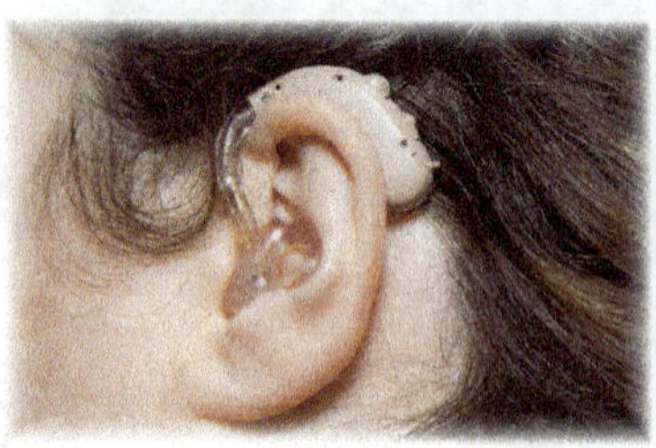

> If you, like me, are hearing impaired,
> And you, like me, have not really cared;
> Beware! Today you may be feeling sane,
> But your hearing loss is affecting your brain.

If you have a hearing loss, you're not alone. Hearing loss is one of the most prevalent chronic conditions affecting older and middle-aged Americans today. And most people with hearing loss don't use hearing aids.*

Count me in. Approximately twelve years ago, I suffered what felt like a stroke but turned out to be an immune system dysfunction, which left me with a 90% hearing loss in my right ear. Delayed steroid injections restored about 40% of that loss.

Through all of this, my husband maintained my problem was not with "hearing" as much as with "listening."

I tried hearing aids for a while, but I was so frustrated with their complexity, constant ringing, and ineffectiveness, I threw them away. I adjusted to the loss. My hearing seemed adequate.

Then I met Ellen Haggarty. She has lived with severe hearing loss since she was four. For sixty years, she's experimented with multiple hearing aid technology and coping strategies. As chair of the Rotarians for Hearing Action Group, she shares this information and her personal experience with people, especially children, all over the world.

When I shared my experience with Ellen, she was adamant: "You must treat your hearing loss," she warned, "untreated hearing loss is linked with accelerated brain tissue loss and dementia, among other things."

Results of a study, conducted by Johns Hopkins Hospital, corroborates Ellen's belief:**

The study found that although the brain tends to shrink with age, its shrinkage seems to increase in older adults who have hearing loss. Because the brain is not receiving auditory stimulation from the deficient ear, it atrophies and can lead to cognitive impairment and Alzheimer's disease. The strain of decoding sounds over many years may overwhelm the brains of those with hearing loss leaving them more vulnerable to dementia.

The research had more to say about the social, psychological, and functional effects of hearing loss; however, I'd read enough.

I've had my hearing reevaluated. I'm now using a new and improved hearing aid. Here's my advice: if you are hearing impaired, or know of someone who is, get help.***

Now that I have hearing aids that work, communication with my husband has improved, right? Wrong. He still maintains I need "listening" aids…

* www.ncoa.org

** https://www.hopkinsmedicine.org/health/wellness-and-prevention/the-hidden-risks-of-hearing-loss

*** For an affordable breakthrough digital hearing aid, with features previously available only on hearing aids costing thousands of dollars, visit MD Hearing Aid online – the doctor's choice for an affordable hearing aid, given positive reviews by the Wall Street Journal, Fox News, Chicago Sun-Times, and Chicago Tribune.

"Dogs are not our whole life, but they make our lives whole." Roger Caras

Maggie May was Seven

Maggie May died when she was seven.

She left us much too soon.

She was the love, the light of my life.

She died on a waning moon.

I've heard it said that if Number Seven

Comes knocking at your door,

Angels are sending you a message

(So listen up)

They'll speak in a whisper, not a roar.

Long ago, angels came down at Christmas

Announcing Jesus's birth.

Do they know Maggie died when she was seven?

Will they come again to visit me on Earth?

As I ponder the likelihood of a visit

In the pain of my loss, in my grief

I'm learning that Number Seven is quite special indeed,

It's amazing, beyond belief.

If I was asked to choose a number,

A number of vast significance.

I'd choose the Number Seven –

The number of perfection and completeness.

God created the world in six days

And rested on Day Seven.

He declared everything He made was good

On earth and up in heaven.

In every major religion, seven is significant,

There are seven candles in the Jewish Menorah.

The Koran claims there are seven heavens

And Muslims walk seven times around the Kaala in Mecca.

The number seven is mentioned 735 times in the scriptures.

A newborn rises and takes seven steps in Buddhism.

Christians believe seven equals the 4 corners of the Earth plus the Trinity

And there are seven worlds in Hinduism.

There are seven holes in your head. (count them!)

Your body has two (inner) and five (outer) layers of skin.

The male body has seven parts.

Without a conscience, you'd likely commit one of the seven deadly sins.

Seven is the basis of myth and folklore.

It's the "most" prime and popular of numbers.

People who spot three stacks of seven side by side,

Shriek with delight and grab their buckets of quarters.

Do, re, mi, fa, sol, la, ti, do are the seven notes we sing.

Ocean waves move in groups of seven;

Counting the inside, a cube has seven dimensions

And seven classical planets orbit the heavens.

Since Maggie May died when she was seven,

The number has a personal significance for me.

I'm still waiting and praying to see if the angels

Will make a special delivery.

(In the meantime, I continue my litany)

ROY G. BIV helps us remember the order

Of the seven colors in a rainbow.

When we see the sunshine after a rain

We remember God's promise of long ago.

There are seven hills in Jerusalem,

In Rome and Istanbul.

In Covey's *Seven Habits of Highly Effective People*,

We find wisdom we didn't learn in school.

There are seven dwarfs in *Sleeping Beauty.*

Sleepy, hands down, is my favorite.

Though he's almost always falling asleep

He's still the most logical and observant.

When the forest animals interrupt work in the mine,

Even though Sleepy isn't thought to be bright,

He realizes the Evil Queen is plotting harm

To the fair-haired and vulnerable Snow White.

There are seven letters in the Roman Numeral system

It's the sum of the opposite sides of dice; two die

Seven is usually found in winning lottery tickets

But break a mirror and you're in for seven years of bad luck, no lie.

With this vast array of examples,

It should be plain for all to see

That seven is special, but if there are angels, where are they

Do they have a message for me?

Then one day it comes with barely a whisper:

"The one you loved, the one who loved you most –

She'll live in your heart and soul forever,

For what is real can never be lost."

Maggie May died when she was seven.

She left us much too soon.

She brought joy and laughter to my life.

She died in the waning moon.

Maximus – a Good Therapy Dog

"An animal's eyes have the power to speak a great language." Martin Buber

"Good morning Lena," I call as Max and I enter her room. Lena is a resident in a local assisted living facility, where Maximus, my yellow Labrador Retriever, and I are visiting. Max wags his tail in greeting. Lena, what is left of her at 90, is sitting up in bed, her head barely clearing the bedcovers.

Her eyes light up when she sees Max. I don't mind that she acknowledges him before greeting me. It's understood that Max is the main act; I'm the sideshow.

I open the blinds to let in some spring sunshine and then get to the task at hand. Max knows the routine. He lies down by the side of the bed and gives me that look: *Hey, it's a hard job, but someone has to do it.*

"What's for breakfast?" I ask Lena, noting the breakfast tray hovering in front of her. Lena is essentially bedridden and opts to eat in her room. My job is to feed her and get as much nutrition into her fragile frame as possible.

While I feed Lena, Max lifts his head, his nose aquiver with the potpourri of smells wafting his way. After a few spoonfuls of oatmeal, Lena loses interest. "What about this coffee cake?" I ask. "Oh, I'll save it for later," she says, so I set the cake on her bedside table and remove the tray so we can talk. At the word "cake," Max lifts his head. I should have noticed...

I rearrange her pillows so she can sit back comfortably and then pull up a chair. We're chatting, when Lena, making a point, absentmindedly pats the bedcovers. That is all the invitation Max needs. With one leap he bounds up from the floor and lands, PLOP, all 100 lbs of him, on top of Lena! Thinking she's suffocated, I desperately pull him away. Where is she? I am about to ring for a nurse when I hear a faint wheezing sound coming from under the heap of bedcovers and pillows. Lena, barely visible, has a huge smile on her face. The wheezing sounds are chuckles.

Relieved, I straighten her out as best I can. "Are you alright?" I ask.

"I haven't had a good laugh like that in a long time," she wheezes. "Good boy," she says stroking Max's silky golden fur. *Good boy? Really?*

When it's time to go, Max jumps down and an exhausted Lena settles in for a nap. I straighten up the room and we leave. Walking down the hall, I notice a distinct cluster of crumbs on Max's nose.

Max, majestic as ever, looks straight ahead. *Don't even ask...*

Emily Dickinson knew dogs well when she observed, "Dogs are better than human beings because they know, but do not tell."

On another occasion, I'm playing the piano for the residents, during their lunch hour. I tether Max to a nearby chair. Suddenly a fire alarm goes off. Max stiffens. For all his 100 pounds, grand name, and majestic bearing, Max is a wimp. Beeping smoke alarms, sirens, and high-frequency sounds send him into panic mode. At home, during a thunderstorm, he hides under the desk downstairs in my husband's office – as far away as he can get from the noise.

Now there's concern in his eyes. I start packing up when the director comes by. "False alarm," she explains, so I continue playing, but when the alarm sounds again, Max lets out a yelp. He is done. "Oh, please stay," the director soothes, "I'll go find out what the problem is. There's no fire drill scheduled for today. Please stay."

Max is quivering by now and giving me worried looks. An aide promises to keep an eye on him, so I return to the piano. I'm well into my concert of hymns and oldies when the alarm sounds a third time. *Really?* I stop playing and look across the room for Max. He is nowhere to be seen.

Finally, I spot him. He is heading for an exit, painstakingly pulling the chair along with him. When I free him, he looks at me, raw fear in his eyes. *I don't know about the rest of you, Mum, but I'm getting out of here.*

Max was just a pup when we started volunteering for Hospice. One of my first assignments was answering the phone. Max was in training then and the staff loved him. He was allowed free rein of the building. And he reigned. Once he returned to my desk with a Campbell's soup can stuck on his nose. He had a hard time explaining that one. Another time he emptied the garbage can in the staff room and finished off a big Mac value meal. To his credit, he left the condiments.

But Max outdid himself at Millie's birthday party. She's invited a few friends to her room to celebrate her 95th birthday. Max and I stop by with a card and balloon. As the birthday girl passes around slices of cake, one of her friends says, "Millie, where's my cake? You gave me an empty plate." I look at Max. He's staring straight ahead. "No matter," coos the hostess, unphased. "Here's another piece." She winks at me. That says it all.

No wonder Max loved therapy work. Hanging around, just being himself. How hard was that? The people adored him. And the payoffs were huge.

That was Max. He was a good therapy dog.

Note: This story was published initially as a series of four separate articles.

Whispers, Words, and Wails – Remembering a Great Dog

"God whispers to us in our pleasures, speaks in our conscience, but shouts in our pains; it is His megaphone to rouse a deaf world." C.S. Lewis

Introduction

Maximus Aurelius, my yellow Labrador retriever, died in August 2000. I don't know the exact time he died in minutes and seconds, *Chronos* time, but the moment he stopped breathing is etched in my memory. It was a moment out of time – a *Kairos* moment.

Maximus was twelve and a half when he died. That's considered by some to be a ripe old age for a Labrador, but he wasn't old enough for me. We made a deal he'd be there for my seventieth birthday and that was two years off. I wasn't ready for him to go. Not that I ever would have been. He was my buddy, my soul mate, the love of my life. I adored him. He was my Max; I was his Mum. He enriched my life. He gave presence and presents. And I'm not the only one grieving his passing.

Max's life with me began as a Paws with a Cause puppy. My job was to provide basic obedience training and socialization for a year, after which time, I'd return him to the center for more rigorous training as a Paws service dog for the handicapped and hearing-impaired. Wanting Max to do well, I threw myself into his training with utter abandon, not realizing that I was bonding with him all the while. When the time came to return him to the center, I was devastated. While I wanted him to be a good service dog, I didn't want to give him up, so completely had he stolen my heart and the hearts of so many he had touched during his training.

My son and daughter rode with me on the day of his return. We cried as we said our goodbyes to a magnificent dog. I'll never forget the moment we signed the papers and said farewell. As a staff member led Max away, he turned to me with a soulful look: *"Hey, Mum, aren't you forgetting something – me?"*

We wept all the way home. Max's absence screamed "Vacancy" everywhere – in the house, the woods, where we walked, the places and people we visited, and most of all, in my heart.

Life limped along and then after a week, I received a call from the Paws trainer." I have bad news and perhaps good news," he said. He went on to explain that Max hadn't passed his initial test and they had decided not to invest any more money and time into his training. The breeder, who had first dibs on him, had declined to take him back. Did I want him? *Did I want him*? I couldn't get there fast enough. Within an hour I had my dog back. On the way, I'd called my mom to tell her the good news. She had bonded with Max too."I've been praying you would get him back," she confessed, somewhat sheepishly. She knew how much I loved him.

It was a joyous reunion. Thinking about the episode, I believe Max knew all along that he'd come back to me. I found out later that during his examination, Max had nipped the veterinarian. He was repentant, to a degree. *"Sorry, Mum, but I had to do it. How else was I going to get back to you?"* I've wondered if the nipping hadn't worked, what Max would have done next to ensure his freedom.

He'd been rejected as a service dog; however, I knew from the training and socialization we'd done, that Max had a powerful influence on people. We became certified as a therapy dog team.

As a Hospice/Therapy dog, Max accompanied me to schools, hospitals, senior centers, and Hospice houses. He had the cushiest job in the world – lying around making people feel good. His interaction with people was potent; all the more so because he was totally oblivious to the power of his presence.

Max outlived my mom, but during her last years, when she was physically helpless and homebound, Max and I visited her often. Max did his best therapy work with her. My mom loved nice things and was meticulous about her house, so I was horrified one day when Max lifted his leg and peed on her houseplant. She just smiled and patted his head. She adored him. I think she always felt a sense of gratification that her prayers brought him back into our lives.

The night before she died, Max and I slept in the living room near the Hospice bed, where she laid. In the middle of the night, Max barked at something he heard outside."Oh, Max, what is it?" my mom croaked weakly. Those were the last words she spoke. She died the next morning.

Lena will miss him too. Max and I stopped by her room during our visits to the assisted living facility where she was a resident. Once, on our way out, he swiped a piece of cake off a plate on her bedside table with an elegant furtive swipe, even I had to admire. We were chatting another time when Lena inadvertently patted the covers to make a point. That was all the invitation Max needed. He leaped onto the bed, nearly suffocating her. What I thought were moans turned out to be spasms of laughter. "I haven't had this much fun in a long time," she gasped, hugging Max. Comedy Central…

Max's death left holes in my life I doubt will ever be filled. Through the holes, my grief spills out in torrents. How many bottles would it take to contain the tears I've shed over the loss of this dog? His magnificent face, his winsome eyes, often harboring a hint of worry, delicately arched brows, soft, velvety ears that smelled like corn muffins, and a wag-wag tail that spoke volumes.

Memories of our times together – the woods where we walked, the beach where he swam and fetched, the spot at the foot of the stairs where he slept, the mudroom where he ate and lapped water, the porch where we had our morning coffee, the front yard where he did his business, the sidewalk where he waited for me to come home and surveyed the neighborhood – his absence screams "Vacancy." Forget the bottles. The tears I've wept over his loss would fill buckets.

I wonder if my grief is excessive, perhaps indicating an instability or emotional imbalance. Dealing with his loss continues to change and shape my life. As I weep, I marvel at the power of our relationship; the hold this dog had on me; the mystery of the bond that bound us together in life and continues to bind us in death.

My feelings aren't unique. A friend confessed that he cried more over the death of his dog than he did when his mother died. Another friend wiped away tears as he described the death of his pet spaniel seven years earlier. I feel their pain.

One thing I know: my bond with Max brought me closer to God than all the years I spent going to church or reading scripture. Because of him, I've heard God's whispers, His words, and His wails.

I. God *whispers* to us in our pleasures…

"Look deep into nature and then you will understand everything better." Albert Einstein

I used to say I took Max for walks. I even bragged about how intelligent he was, for when I picked up the leash, he'd head for the door and I'd take him for a walk. For many years I thought this was the way it was. But now, older and wiser, I realize that Max walked me. Those walks changed my life.

Max taught me an awareness of the simple subtle pleasures of nature. He was always on the alert and because I was completely attuned to him, his awareness transferred to me. I discovered the world of nature through his eyes and ears.

When a squirrel frisked across our path, Max made a mad dash in pursuit just for the fun of it. After a good hard spurt, he'd return panting and laughing. *Life is good, Mum!* If he was on-leash, he'd stiffen and tug at his restraint. *Aw, life isn't fair.* In his later years, on leash or off, he'd pause, look longingly, and move on. *Just a squirrel, Mum…*

He taught me to love and enjoy birds – Dickinson's "things with feathers," and "symbols of hope." A red-bellied sapsucker flitting through the trees, a pesky blue jay with its piercing, "jay, jay, jay," a cardinal with its conspicuous crest, calling out its morning, "cheer, cheer, cheer," prompted Max's tail to wag in pure joy of the moment.

Hanging out on the back porch one afternoon, we heard a pounding sound in the trees. A pileated woodpecker was drumming, forging the square holes for which they're famous. Max listened awhile and then lifted his head. *Is this guy for real Mum?* As the drumming continued, he glanced my way with a pensive, knowing, hopeful look. *What is taking her so long?* Max was no dummy when it came to the birds and bees. He knew the male was drumming for his she-bird.

Kicking up a white-tailed deer in the woods always put Max on full alert. He knew these guys were special. In the foolishness and rambunctiousness of youth, he was hot for a chase, but as he aged, he'd just watch the white tails disappear into the foliage and walk on. *Conserving energy, Mum.* Not that Max would have chased anything for the kill. It was all a game; his romp with nature.

He especially loved going to Lake Michigan. When we arrived at the intersection of trails in the woods called "Four Corners," he'd invariably pull towards the path that led to the beach. *Can we go to the beach today Mum, please?* If he was lucky, he'd pick up the pace, wagging his tail in anticipation of fishy smells, lapping waves, and bobbing tennis balls.

At the beach, he cools his belly in the water and wriggles his nose in the air. *I'm ready Mum! Let 'er rip!* Fetching is on! He spots the ball even when the sun, sparkling and glinting on the waves, makes it hard to see. Off he goes, muscling his golden body through the water, his eyes focused on the bobbing prize. He lunges for the ball, gulping in a mouthful of water in the process. Then back he comes, plowing through the current with his masterful doggie paddle. All I can see of this glistening golden wonder is his magnificent head just above the water, his eyes glued on me. He rides the crest of the waves until his front legs touch the sand. *Yup! Life is a beach!* He drops the ball at my feet and we start over. He'll never stop.

Remembering these moments makes Max's presence so tangible, the tears begin flowing and my throat starts to ache.

How many times have I buried my head in that soft furry coat and inhaled the scent of him – an experience so palpable, I can smell him still. How many times, tickling his soft belly, while engulfing his huge golden frame in a body hug, did I whisper into his ear, "Oh, Max, what will I do without you?"

I'm finding out. As I walk our familiar haunts, I sense his presence – calming, reassuring, and peaceful. Ever loyal, he was always there for me.

It wasn't always this way. In truth, Max and I were a study in opposites when we went for walks. Max was always eager to hit the trails, straining at the leash, wagging his tail, eyes alight with anticipation of nature's sights, sounds, and sniffs. *Yippee! Let's go, Mum!* I, on the other hand, was oblivious to nature's bounty, a natural worrier, deep into my mind, bogged down with the heavy baggage of thoughts, emotions, and problems of the day. I was drawn to problems like Max was drawn to marrow bones! What a pair we made. How did Max manage to maintain his joyfulness and sanity living with me?

Over time though, the influence of Max's serene presence instilled a sense of peace and eased the cares and burdens that weighed me down. The precious hours spent with Max, in nature, wrought a profound change in me. I'm more reflective and introspective; less in need of words and more at peace with silence; more aware of the inner noise of thoughts streaming through my head and the outer noise around me; more in tune with inner stillness and external silence.

The stillness I experience is not merely an absence of noise. It is a power itself; an intelligence beyond thought. I realize that every created entity came into being from nothing and took on form and shape from a vast underlying unconsciousness.

"And the world was without form and void…God created the world and it was good." It matters not to me if creation took the literal seven days or billions of evolutionary years.

In a squirrel's exuberance, the call of a jay, the flitting of a sapsucker, the lapping of the waves, and the bounding leaps of a white-tail, is a simplicity beyond complexity. It's a truth I do not understand, but one I've come to know.

It dawns on me that I am one with all of nature; one with the essence of every living thing. The vastness of space, out of which the world was created and which enfolds all of nature, also holds and enfolds me. Tears spring to my eyes. My heart contracts, like a brace of birds. *"Woof, woof, Mum!"* This deep ache I feel connects me with Max. As painful as it is, I don't want the ache to go away because it connects me with him.

This connection, strangely enough, seems more poignant in his absence than it was in his presence. In his absence, I commune with him on a profound spiritual level. In this place of stillness, I can never lose him. The adage is true: nothing real is ever lost.

Woof! Do you hear it, Mum? The silence? The stillness?
Indeed I do. And out of the stillness comes a whisper:
"Be still and know that I am God…" *Psalm 46:10*

II. God *speaks* in our conscience...

"No self. No problem." Buddhist Master

There was more to learn. As Max and I walked the trails in the woods, I came to appreciate the bounties of nature in yet another way. A towering tree, a budding leaf, a swooping, diving owl, a clump of beach grass waving gracefully in the wind, a cloud billowing overhead, and my beloved Maximus, nose to the ground, reading his daily newspaper, his tail wagging in the ecstasy of the moment. Everything was so completely itself, so surrendered, and so alive. *I am, Mum! I am!* What is Max trying to tell me?

Entering nature's sanctuary, bogged down with my burdensome baggage of thoughts and worries, I felt somewhat like an alien; an interloper in their world.

The creatures of nature live totally in the present while I am imprisoned in the past, feeling guilt, and rehashing experiences. They are at peace, while I am compulsively preoccupied with the future, seeking to add to my life, to make it more complete.

They embody stillness and serenity while I am plagued by noise. Thoughts race wildly through my head. I have a life story – a "me," while they are simply and completely themselves. Freed from a self-concept, an ego, they exist with humility and dignity. I longed to be more like them.

You can, Mum, you can! Max's wag-wag tail was all encouraging.

Under Max's tutelage, I begin listening to the voice in my head, curious about the thoughts streaming through my mind, like a babbling brook. I begin to observe my life story – the "me," made up of details occurring between the dates of my birth and my death. I visualize those dates engraved on my tombstone and realize that the details of my life – the "me" – will be summarized, one day, by a mere dash between those dates.

Though the details of my life, any life, for that matter, are interesting, they cannot be its essence. There is a deeper dimension of consciousness to be found – a dimension beyond thought; a presence, an awareness known by all natural beings, which I long to realize myself. *Woof, woof, Mum! You're getting there!*

I sense that hints of this deeper spiritual dimension have something to do with Max. I continue listening to the mental noise and hear troubling things. The voice in my head speaks of insecurity, envy, fear, prejudice, defensiveness, resentment, bitterness, victimization, complaining, and reactivity – patterns that often resulted in conflicts and verbal clashes with others.

With a new sense of awareness, I watch as the past events of my life are projected onto the screen of my mind's eye. Sadly, there's no popcorn for this video.

I watch a little girl, growing up on a small farm, in west Michigan. Shortly after she is born – the sixth of seven children – her father is diagnosed with rheumatic fever. Her mother, unable to cope with caring for her husband, five children, a new baby, and the added burden of chores, asks a neighbor to help care for her newborn. The baby, however, not realizing her parents' plight, wants her mother to feed her, to hold her, and rock her to sleep at night. She cries constantly, adding to her mother's burdens. Never bonding with her mother, the little girl seeks her attention by crying as an infant and rebelling as she grows older. Feelings of insecurity plague her throughout her life.

The scene on the screen changes. I am with a friend, who is sharing her marital problems. Having gone through a divorce myself, I'm empathetic, yet I watch, in distaste, as a subtle feeling of satisfaction invades my empathy and concern. I seem to enjoy knowing she is experiencing the hell I've known; assuaging my pain through her difficulties.

Next, I watch a young woman having dinner with her parents, discussing points of dogma. Having joined a progressive church, she attempts to undermine their literal views of scripture with her newly-found liberal ones. I watch, dismayed, as my father – a meek and humble man, whose faith has seen him through the rigors of living and working the land, the death of a daughter, and the estrangement of a son, who survived the jungles of Viet Nam, but never returned home – notes quietly, "I'm going to believe what the bible teaches." He withdraws from the fray to his favorite chair in the living room.

It seems I need desperately to be right. I watch myself in several confrontational battles, where I, cleverly and smugly, seek to come out the winner in religious arguments, political discussions, and tennis matches.

I am constantly in a state of "doing," with everything done as a means to an end. I appear frantic and fearful, often irritated and impatient with others. Where was the joy, the peace, the creative fulfillment, the promise of life?

Quick to judge and evaluate, I see myself, in one particularly appalling scenario, listening to gossip about an acquaintance, adding salacious comments of my own.

In the aftermath of a hellish divorce, I take my feelings of resentment and victimization out on others, careening through relationships, like the proverbial bull, causing additional hurt and pain.

The following scenes would have been comical if they hadn't been so dysfunctional: In the first scene, I am driving down the highway when a driver passes me and cuts me off. "What do you think you're doing?" I mutter. I accelerate and tailgate him to show my displeasure. Next, I'm having lunch out with a friend. When my spinach salad is delivered, I dig in, only to put down my fork, grumbling, "How can they serve this soggy stuff and call it spinach?" I hail a waitress and demand that she take it back. In the final scene, I'm in my doctor's office. Impatient with having to wait, I sigh and sputter, "How rude! Doesn't the doctor know I'm a busy person too?"

Thankfully, like a giant Etch-a-Sketch, the screen clears, and a faint white aura envelops the space. The same three scenes play out a second time, but now, instead of personalizing the events, creating a "me" against "them" conflict, I deftly defuse the ego, by stating simply, "He cut me off," "This spinach is soggy," and "I guess the doctor is having a busy day." I have to smile. The Buddhist master had it right: "No self, no problem."

As the movie comes to an end, I am dazed and shaken. I dislike the character I've seen. I dislike myself! Then, through my shame, comes a sudden stab of insight: I've been acting out of an unconsciousness of the truths I am now beginning to learn and understand. I did the best I could at the time. I can forgive myself and those who have hurt me, for they too were acting out of similar selfish motives.

A sense of freedom comes over me. It's as though I've escaped from a prison whose bars are constructed merely of thoughts. Just becoming aware of the thoughts and their ability to affect and control my life is liberating.

The truth is, we are larger than our limited thoughts, actions, and perspectives; larger than our egos. We are part of a unified whole, where all things are interwoven and nothing exists in or by itself.

The words of Jesus come to mind: "Forgive them for they know not what they do," and I know they're meant for me and for those who have hurt me.

A deep sense of awareness envelops me. I feel a kinship with nature, a oneness with human beings, and a space, where, acting out of stillness, instead of thoughts and ego, every encounter becomes sacred.

Woof, woof! Isn't it wonderful, Mum? Being free? It's Max, breaking into my reverie.

There was never any ego muddying up our relationship was there Max. I'll never be as wild and free as you, but now, at least, I'm aware of the ego and its power. It can no longer hold me captive.

And then I hear the voice. It is clear and oh so sweet:

"Do onto others as you would have them do onto you." *Luke 6:31*

Woof!

III. God *shouts* in our pain…

"An animal's eyes have the power to speak a great language." Martin Buber

There was a final lesson to be learned, and, as it turned out, Max would give his life, to ensure I got this point.

Life was always abundant in the woods, but during the summer Max died, I noticed that death was there too. Toppled trees, languished leaves, and scarred stumps were uneasy reminders that life doesn't last forever.

I suppose I noticed these signs of deterioration and decay because Max was slowing down. There was no denying it. He'd had a couple of seizures the previous year (which the vet assured me were normal – how can a seizure be normal?), he'd stopped eating (unheard of for a lab), and he seemed short of breath. Even then, he got dressed and showed up for work every day. *Don't worry Mum. I'm okay.* But he wasn't. Something was wrong.

Our walks slowed down that summer, but, Max wanted to go to the beach, so that's what we did, resting frequently along the way. We played fetch like we always did, though now, I walked out to the sand bar with him and threw balls from there. He knew the routine was off. *What are you doing out here Mum? I don't need a handicap. I'm good.*

His dogged determination to keep the routine broke my heart. Once I threw the ball too far and stood there, with my heart in my mouth, as he struggled to get back. His breath came in ragged jaggy gasps. After that, I threw the ball, ever so carefully, just over his head, but even so, I held my breath until he was back on a firm footing. His loyalty knew no bounds.

The outings became excruciatingly painful, but as long as he was willing to keep it up, I had all the time in the world. He'd stand and look longingly at his food, but he wouldn't eat. When thyroid medication and arthritis injections didn't work, my vet was stumped and surrendered him up to old age. Little did we know that he was bleeding internally and gravely ill.

As it turned out Max had an enlarged spleen and needed emergency surgery. He survived the surgery but died at home the next day. No wonder he couldn't eat – the spleen, the surgeon removed, was the size of a football. It was amazing that he'd lived as long as he did with such a massive obstruction and loss of blood.

The day he died is etched in my memory. Author Madeline L'Engle writes that no one, animal or human, should die alone, so it's small comfort, that I was with him as he drew his final breath.

When he collapsed on that fateful day, I laid with him in the library. His breathing was slow and irregular. My mind was in a panic, torn between trying to get him emergency help and not wanting to leave him, lest he die without me. Suddenly he emitted a deep guttural sound, raised his head, and stared at me with a burning heartrending gaze. *Thanks for letting me be your dog, Mum! I love you!* I thought then he might recover, but instead, he collapsed and in seconds he stopped breathing. Those were the last words he uttered.

His luxurious furry body quickly began to harden, but I couldn't tear myself away from him. My children were with me, and my son took charge, insisting that we bury Max immediately. Moving as if in a dream, I gave him up, found a shovel, and went with my son to pick out a burial site. Weeping, he began shoveling and spewing sand.

Frantic thoughts flitted through my mind. It was good Max was dead because burying him alive would be horrible; a deep grave was good, for it would keep wild animals from digging him up; burying him was better than losing him in the woods (as had happened a few weeks earlier), and never knowing what had happened to him.

My son handed me the shovel and I snapped back to reality. In shock, I stared at the deep gaping hole that would be Max's final resting place. I watched, horrified, as my children lowered his lifeless body into the ground. We returned him to the earth wrapped in his favorite woolen blanket. I threw the first shovelful of sand, gently, ever so gently, on his body. It was one of the hardest things I have ever done. A silent scream rose from deep inside of me. "No! No! No!" The screams continued with each shovelful of sand I cast into the hole. Then it was over. With a heartrending wail, I surrendered him up.

Exhausted, we stood there for a few moments, then, one by one, we paid our final respects to a great dog and drifted away.

It happened so fast – his collapse, death, and burial, it seemed surreal. My family suggested that I lie down but the woods was calling.

For hours my daughter and I wept and walked the trails Max and I had walked and claimed as ours. For the rest of that day, and for days afterward, I lived in a daze. I couldn't get my mind wrapped around the truth that my buddy and best friend was gone.

Time is supposed to take the edge off grief and pain; yet even now, as I stand at his grave, my grief is as raw as it was the day he died. Yet strangely, life goes on – the clock ticks, days turn into weeks, seasons come and go. Soon an entire year has passed then two and three. I carry on with the routines of my life without him.

Yet, over time, my grief has altered. It's this change I must analyze in an attempt to understand the power this dog has on my life. *Woof!* Is this the final lesson Max has to teach me?

I look more closely at those toppled trunks and rotten leaves. I notice something I missed before. The trunks and leaves appear to be dead, but if microorganisms and molecules are at work everywhere, which they are, the rotted materials must be full of life. They will give birth to new life one day themselves. Perhaps there is life here after all… *Getting closer, Mum!*

Then one day, I'm walking Max's favorite trail to the beach, ruing the fact that I hadn't had a chance to say goodbye to him, since he was rushed into surgery, and his last day home, he wasn't himself. Then I remembered. We did have our final time together. *Good for you Mum! You remembered!*

It happened the afternoon of Max's surgery. He hadn't recovered sufficiently for us to take him home, so my husband and I drove him to an emergency animal hospital, forty-five minutes away, where he would spend the night. It was a "nip and tuck" drive and the surgeon wasn't sure he'd make it.

I laid down in the back of the jeep with him, burying my face in his luxurious fur, rubbing his belly, and gently scratching his ears. They still smelled like corn muffins. I looked in those winsome eyes and told him how much I loved him, what a great dog he was, and how I wasn't ready for him to die. I reminded him that I wouldn't be seventy for two more years. My head was pounding so hard, I thought it would burst.

Then, through the pain, a thought skittered through my mind. In the instant I grasped it, my mind cleared. I told Max I didn't want him to suffer, and if it was best, he could die. I would be okay. I thought of something a friend had told me (why it came to me then, I don't know) that dogs who are loved exceedingly much, die sooner. It's as if too much has been required of them. Had I caused Max unnecessary pain and suffering by holding on to him and not wanting him to die? I thought of the way he'd trucked around with me all summer, lugging that huge horrid spleen around. If we'd been able to help him sooner he wouldn't have had to suffer.

Mum! Max's gaze was filled with such pathos, such vulnerability, and surrender, it seared deep into my soul. *No regrets, Mum… One more thing. I chose to suffer Mum – for you.*

He was weak and failing, but his gaze was strong. He was near death, as it turned out, but his eyes were translucent, as though a light was streaming through them from somewhere beyond.

We laid in silence for the remainder of the trip. I didn't want to waste our time on words and anyway there was nothing more to be said.

As I looked into his eyes, a feeling of peace stole over me, like a coverlet on a bed. I sensed his time was up, but I knew his death would be a clean wound and all would be well. The moment was sacred, filled with humility and dignity – and eternity. I could have died and met my Maker then and there.

You and me, Mum – together, forever.

I will always wonder if Max died because I gave him permission, or if he would have kept going if I'd asked him to.

I've reached the beach. I'm alone, but not really, because Max is here, a palpable "presence in the absence," and along with his presence, is something more.

It's the final lesson – a mystery I do not understand, yet I know it to be so: I have met God in the magnificence of a dog. I've found hope in a wag-wag tail. I've heard His voice shouting to me from the depths of a dog's winsome eyes. The words are powerful; the language strange, but not unfamiliar:

"{She} that hath ears to hear, let {her} hear…" *Revelation 2:17*

"Oh death, where is thy sting? Oh, grave, where is thy victory?" *I Corinthians 15:55*

And finally this: "Nothing unreal exists; Nothing real is ever lost." *A Course in Miracles,* Foundation for Inner Peace

"*Woof!*"

Appendix

I. Janet Hasselbring – Author

A. *Tales from Pelican Cove* series

The books in this series feature the wild/shorebirds from FL and beyond and are based on Jan's experiences with these amazing birds, during the time she and her husband, Don, wintered in Sarasota, Florida. Educational, entertaining, and beautifully illustrated, they make great gifts for adults, children, and grandchildren.

Andy Discovers Peanut Butter – Andy the anhinga, is rewarded when he helps Bubba, the blue heron.

What Do You See, Mrs. Night Heron? – Mrs. Heron sees amazing sights while sitting on her nest.

Ossie the Brave Fish Hawk – a tale of bird piracy involving an osprey, a bald eagle, and a horned owl.

Presley's First Day of Fishing – Presley catches his first fish only to have it stolen right out of his pouch.

Mimi the Mimic – based on a poem by Emily Dickinson, a tale of hope and remembrance.

Ruddy: Living on the Wind – follow a turnstone on his migration from Patagonia to the Arctic mudflats.

Can We Nest Here? A Tale of Acceptance and Belonging, inspired by the work of Brene' Brown

B. *Country Dairy* series – *Looking Back, Moving Forward*

Country Dairy: A Week with Hinie and Ellen, a pictorial memoir – Jan describes life on her family farm, in the 1930s when her parents lived and worked on the land.

In the Garden: Ellen, A Memoir – Jan pays tribute to her mother, "an ordinary woman who became extraordinary on the small farm, where, with her husband, Henry, she put down her roots and served her Lord.

II. Janet Hasselbring, Speaker

The Stories behind the Stories – Jan presents the experiences which inspired the books in the series, *Tales from Pelican Cove*, the interesting facts she's learned, and the connections she's made through her writing – a power point presentation.

The Power of Migration – Jan shares the amazing phenomenon of migration, incorporating her two migratory stories, *Mimi and Mimic*, and *Ruddy: Living on the Wind* into a power point presentation.

Can We Nest Here? and the work of Brene' Brown – Jan explains how the work of researcher Brown on acceptance, vulnerability, shame, and connection, inspired her book.

In the Garden, a Memoir – In addition to reviewing/discussing her mother's extraordinary story, Jan examines the power of prayer, the genre of memoir, and the unique challenges of writing personal story. Perfect for a women's bible studies, book clubs, retreats, or an informal get together. "Janet Hasselbring is a wonderful storyteller! When you're 'in the garden,' with Jan's mother and God, their conversations could easily be your own. Pour yourself a cup of coffee, sit on the front porch, and get ready to be inspired by the story of this remarkable follower of Jesus." Clare De Graf, *The 10 Second Rule*

Country Dairy: Looking Back, Moving Forward – through her pictorial memoir, Jan shares experiences growing up on the farm, describes how the farm has changed since she lived there, and pays tribute to her parents' hard work, dedication, and perseverance.

Book clubs – Tweets is an excellent read for book clubs and discussion groups. If you belong to a book club and decide to use Tweets, Jan will give your members a discounted price. She's also available to read and discuss various stories in the book and examine the short story's particular genre – Jan's favorite writing medium. Several quotes used in the book make great discussion topics.

III. For more information about Jan and her books, visit janethasselbring.wordpress.com. and https://www.facebook.com/JanHAuthor. To contact Jan: janethasselbring23@gmail.com

Tweeting for Charity:

Every year Jan's direct sales profits of Tweets (approximately $5.00 per book), will be donated equally among these charities: Humanity for Prisoners and the Innocence Project, Country Dairy, Gulu, Uganda Mission Project, St. Mary's Food Pantry, The Nature Conservancy, The Audubon Society, and a dog rescue/shelter, such as Noah's Project, Michele's Rescue, or Pound Buddies.

Acknowledgements

Cheryl Tomas –

I am indebted to Cheryl, a computer/software techie, whose technical prowess made this book possible. Her attention to detail, her ability to problem-solve, and her commitment to excellence know no bounds. On a personal note, Cheryl's calm, no-panic demeanor, sense of humor, and dependability make her a pleasure to work with. There is no problem she cannot solve; she gets the job done.

Michelle Fields –

Michelle's professional leadership, as editor of Senior Perspectives Newspapers and her support and encouragement to us, writers, is invaluable. She is a cheerleader, a mentor, and a friend. Without her leadership, I would not have a venue for my writing. Thank you Michelle. You are an amazing person!

My husband, Donald -

When I shift into writing mode, it can't be easy, and for your support, understanding, and especially your patience, thank you. Many a dinner hour has been pushed back toward the Evening News or abolished entirely, while I pursue an idea "down a rabbit hole," conduct a raid on pesky useless words, or fret through a writing deadline. I wouldn't want to live with myself; however, you do it with kindness and grace. Thank you.